Down Right

GOOD

Down Right GOOD

KAREN KELLY BOYCE

KFR
Communications, LLC

Down Right Good

First printing, 2011

Copyright © 2011 by Karen Kelly Boyce

Published by: KFR Communications, LLC
148 Hawkin Rd
New Egypt, NJ 08533

Publisher's Note: The author and publisher have taken care in preparation of this book but make no expressed or implied warranty of any kind and assume no responsibility for errors or omissions. No liability is assumed for incidental or consequential damages in connection with or arising out of the use of the information contained herein.

ISBN-10: 0-9828-9591-7
ISBN-13: 978-0-982-89591-7

Printed in the United States of America

www.kfrcommunications.com

This novel is dedicated to my son, Michael
John Patrick. I pray that you will
always be open to Christ in the unexpected
places and faces of the world.

On a horse full of thunder, with a sword flaming bright
They knew their Messiah would be a man full of might
Leaders scanned the temple for the god of the Strong
And many just followed on this path proved so wrong

In a dark, remote village as a babe in a stall
Was the true face of God, so dependent and small
Crying out for his mother, with no strength in his call
And the world went on spinning with no notice at all

Mike, today is no different, as the haughty world looks
For the man of the tongue or the best-selling book
For the man of great wealth, counting gold in his dreams
Or the man of great power making war with his schemes
Strutting proud on the TV – mixing truth with great lies –
Watch the dancing, false prophets weaving webs that will tie

But He still comes today, and son, He comes as He wills
In the eyes of the poor and the cries of the ill
In the small gentle steps of the man with the cane
In the face of the starving and the blush of the shamed
In the refugee's tent and the prisoner's cell
In the face most rejected, most ignored, and repelled
In the prayers of the broken and the dream of the slave
There you'll find Jesus Christ, as He empties each grave

Contents

With special appreciation for
Linda DeGregory
for her editing skills and
wonderful friendship.

With special gratitude to
Sue Anderson Gioulis
for her amazing cover illustration.

With special thanks to
Louise Barton,
a fellow writer,
for her advice and guidance.

One

Behind and before you encircle me and rest your hand upon me. Such knowledge is beyond me, far too lofty for me to reach. (Psalm 139:5-6)

The morning light had a strange bend, as if the world was proclaiming a change, a transformation of the ordinary. The slant of sunlight through the blinds of Angie's window woke her with a feeling of oddity. In the dawning of awareness, she sensed something big was going to happen.

She knew she had slept later than usual, but this peculiar sensation reflected more than delay, much more than a different angle of sun. She had no words for the feeling. Angie was born with Down's syndrome, an extra chromosome, and had a limited vocabulary even on an ordinary day. Her mind held no words for the unusual. When fully awake, the feeling still lingered.

Yet, as if to call her instincts a lie, the routine of washing, dressing, and grooming were mundane. Even the house called her intuition dishonest. The house spoke of routine. The air smelled of Saturday waffles. The step on the top of the stairs creaked and today was no different. Within minutes, she forgot the feeling of distinctiveness the day promised, but her forgetting did not negate the prophecy.

In her forgetting, ten-year-old Angie rushed, pouncing in

canvas sneakers. She bolted through the front door and stopped at the bundle on the porch. Winded, she inhaled the February air and stood looking up the avenue, past the older homes that lined the quiet street. She felt confused and the feeling stayed her. She stood pouting for a minute, unable to decide what to do.

Sometimes, when she had trouble gathering her thoughts, she would have to pause, waiting for her mind to catch up to an alteration in the usual. Angie loved routine. Anything that changed the customary confused her. She liked to wave at the jovial truck driver because he would always smile and wave back.

Angie also loved the angel that guarded the rotund driver. That angel was plumb and round-faced. He looked like the truck driver and was usually laughing, just like the driver. She had always been able to see the angels that protected others.

Angie's grandmother, Moma, had explained it once, saying, it was as if God had an equal measure of grace for His creation. She thought God may have taken some quickness from Angie's mind so he could give her the grace to see these heavenly creations. When they smiled at her, Angie was tempted to talk to them. She had learned not to do this.

When she was younger, she thought everyone could see the angels. She soon learned better. People couldn't see angels and thought she was odd or even crazy when she talked to the unseen entities. Moma had taught her to only talk to the angels when no one else was around.

She missed the truck because she overslept. Moma had told her to get to bed last night, but Angie given her a hard time. Lying on her stomach in front of the TV, she remained engrossed by the stars walking on the red carpet of the promenade. Flashing bulbs from the cameras sparkled against the starlets' sequined gowns. She thought it looked like the fireflies she caught and placed in Mason jars each summer.

Angie held her breath in anticipation as each nomination was announced. She clapped her palms together, rolling on the floor in eagerness as the winner climbed to the stage. She had not seen any of the winning films. Angie didn't like movies; she liked cartoons. She fell asleep on the living room floor and vaguely remembered her brother Josh carrying her up the stairs so Moma could tuck her in bed.

She usually sat on the porch waiting for the delivery truck. *Oh well*, thought Angie, tugging the papers inside, *me still glad watch show*. The door slammed as she yanked the bundle into the living room.

"Angie," called Moma, in a raspy voice, "your waffles are ready."

"No time eat!" she answered as she cut the string holding the tabloids together. Angie wanted to fold the papers and be on her way. Saturday was her favorite day. Oh, she liked school all right, but liked Saturdays best.

Moma didn't take no for an answer. "Get in this kitchen and eat your breakfast, young lady. It's a sin to waste food."

Angie sighed, knowing she would have to stop and eat. Moma always made her eat. With a cobbler's apron over her housedress, her grandmother was constantly fussing around in the kitchen. There was, at all times, a large pot of soup on the stove and a loaf of bread rising on the counter.

Only once, did Angie remember the elderly woman taking the apron off and putting on a jacket and skirt. The day the official woman came. Her grandmother called her "the lady from the state" and seemed so nervous about her visit. Even Josh seemed jumpy that day. Angie couldn't understand why – the lady seemed so nice. However, the woman carried a briefcase full of papers and forced her to sit still. Restless, Angie quickly wearied of the woman's questions, endless questions that made her head pound. She was glad when the lady left. Josh and Moma exchanged knowing looks and seemed especially relieved.

"Hurry up, Angie," Moma called. "Josh is using up all the syrup."

She left the papers and was heading to the kitchen, when she heard Moma call, "Did you clean your hands?"

Looking at her hands blackened with ink, Angie rubbed her palms on the thighs of her jeans, "Yeah. Mean - Yes Moma."

Running into the kitchen, she seized the seat next to Josh. She gave her older brother a hard kiss on his cheek. Josh laughed, grabbing the edge of the table to stop a tumble from his chair.

"Whoa, girl, you don't know your own strength," he responded. "Better hurry up, before I eat your waffles."

Angie laughed. "Jessica would love kiss you."

She watched his cheeks flush. "What makes you think she would like to kiss me?"

"She make me a new friend. Like other girls who stare at you. You no know she like you?" The young girl's head tilted as she teased her brother.

"Maybe she just likes you? Did you ever think of that?" Josh replied.

"No, no. She talk all you. No care me. Ask come over to house. Want you be home. She want you, not me." Angie laughed, recalling all the other girls who tried to connect with her brother.

Angie turned and watched Moma as she wiped the waffle iron clean. Struggling, at the age of two, Angie started calling her grandmother rrrrrrrrrma. The surgery Angie received soon after birth repaired the cleft palate, but left a distinct scar on her upper lip. Despite the treatment and weekly speech therapy, she continued to have trouble pronouncing some words. Her word for her grandmother became Moma. The name stuck and now everyone in the small Jersey town knew the old woman by that name.

With her back bent like a pretzel and a large hump between her shoulders, Moma seemed to be looking at the floor. Angie could see the two angels that were always with the old woman. One of the angels always stood behind her grandmother. The angel held her hands out on Moma's sides as if waiting to catch the elderly woman if she fell. Angie thought it seemed wrong. The way her grandmother bent frontward, the young girl was sure that if Moma ever fell, she would fall forward. If this happened, she would fall right onto the second angel who was always before her.

This angel didn't seem to worry about whether the grandmother would fall. He looked ahead, facing the way Moma did. The angel held the handle of a large sword that was stuck in his belt. He wore the suit of an old-time soldier, like the ones Angie had seen on TV. She laughed each time she saw the soldiers wearing the short skirts with metal chest protectors, but this is how the angel in front of her grandmother was dressed. He had a metal helmet and, with eyes darting around, scanned as if ready for a fight. Most people only had one angel, but Moma had two. Maybe, Angie thought, it was because she had to raise two grandchildren.

Having two angels seemed to make Moma brilliant. Angie thought her grandmother was the smartest woman she had ever known. She seemed to know everything, all the poems in the world.

Angie remembered her first day at school. She had been so troubled when Josh had not met her for the walk home. She waited at the corner just as her brother had told her to do, but didn't see him anywhere. She thought he must have forgotten about meeting her. Figuring she knew the way home, she started out on her own. After all, she thought, it only few blocks. She had only walked a block when Tommy Ellis came from behind and knocked her to the ground.

"Look how stupid you are! Ugly!" Tommy shouted. Angie tried to get up, but the older boy pushed her down.

"Get down! After all, you're a down aren't you? My mother says you're a down," the freckled-face boy yelled.

A crowd of kids gathered in a circle to watch. Upset, Angie kept trying to get up but Tommy just kept kicking her to the ground. He started to yell, "You're a down! You're a down!"

Angie could feel her new dress rip as tears streaked her cheeks. The other kids began yelling with Tommy, "You're a down!"

Suddenly, Josh pushed through the crowd of children. "What's going on here?" All the youngsters backed up, but Tommy was too busy tormenting his victim to notice Angie's older brother. Josh picked him up by the front of his shirt and Angie saw the shaken look on Tommy's face. It only took a minute for the girl to start running.

When she had been lying on the ground, she had seen the children's angels standing behind them as the crowd circled her. The angels turned in shame and seemed sad to see what the children were doing to her. Some of the angels wept, but they did not move to stop the taunting. Angie could never see her own angel, but she could feel him holding her as she lay on the sidewalk. Her angel tried to comfort her. She was aware of the angel's love, but had no desire to stay. She ran the two blocks home, her vision blurred by tears.

Bursting through the kitchen door, Angie ran smack into Moma, who caught the beaten child in her arms. "What's wrong?" she asked soothingly, wiping her granddaughter's face with her apron.

"Me a down," Angie sputtered. "Called me a down and not stop!"

"Shh . . . Sit down and take some deep breaths."

She tried to do as Moma said. It was hard to stop her body from shaking. Her respirations slowed. She felt safe now in this familiar kitchen. Taking some sips from the glass of water Moma handed her, Angie told her story. Josh came in the kitchen door as she was finishing. He tried to talk to his little sister, but his grandmother raised her finger to her lips to quiet him.

"I'm afraid it's my fault. I forgot to teach you the poems. Those kids just wanted you to finish the poem."

Stunned, Angie stopped crying and raised an inquisitive face to her grandmother. "What poem? What you mean?"

Moma stroked Angie's hair and gently lifted her face up by the chin. "Why, when those kids were calling you a down, they just wanted you to finish the poem. When they called you a down, you should have answered, 'Yes, I'm downright good.'"

Angie's face filled with wonder. "Me thought making fun of me. Me so different."

Moma smiled. "Well of course you're different. Everyone's

different. No, it's my fault. I forgot to teach you the end of the poem. Whenever someone calls you a down, smile as wide as you can and shout, "Yes, I'm downright good."

Angie was amazed. She hadn't known the kids were just playing with her. School never frightened her again.

When Tommy called her a down the next week, she knew what to do.

She smiled and shouted, "Yes, I'm downright good." All the children laughed and it seemed to confuse her tormenter.

By the time Tommy called her a "tart" the following week, Moma had already taught her the poem. Angie smiled right at him and shouted, "Tarts are sour, tarts are sweet. God made me, so I'm a treat."

Now the other children left her alone. Most of them seemed amused by the answers Angie gave. Tommy seemed angrier. He took every opportunity to attack her. She learned to watch for Tommy, to avoid him. She shivered when she thought of being alone with the hateful boy; however, most of the other children were nice to her by now.

Angie was proud her grandmother knew the poems. Five years ago, during the kindergarten beating, she wouldn't have thought she would like school, but now Angie did. She liked the teachers and the kids. She went to special classes, but knew that everyone was different so it was okay.

Angie started to cough, choking on her last piece of waffle.

"Slow down, squirt!" Josh said as he reached over to pat her back. "Why are you eating so fast?"

Taking a deep sip of orange juice, she answered, "Late fold papers, put in bags and bicycle basket."

"Don't worry. Take your time eating. I don't have baseball practice until nine. I'll help you get the papers ready."

Angie ran over to Josh and flung her arms around him. "Thanks, Josh, I hate be late. People waiting me."

Moma watched the children from across the room. She sighed

at how seriously her granddaughter took her job delivering the free weekly paper. Most people used it for the supermarket coupons. Some liked to laugh at the editorials on the local politicians. Yet, Angie delivered the small tabloid as if everyone's life depended on it. The grandmother had read about children like Angie, children with Down's syndrome. They were usually fastidious about their chores and jobs.

Both Angie and Josh were growing up so quickly. Moma had been raising them since the death of her daughter, Julia, right after Angie's birth. Her son-in- law had taken off, right after hearing the news of his daughter's birth defects. Moma often wondered if he had even looked at the child before he deserted her.

The pain and weariness of her aging body was becoming more pronounced each day. She was worn out and slowing down. If only she could stay to watch them mature. She was fearful of leaving the children too soon, that she would never make the five years it would take for Josh to become eighteen. She especially worried about Angie. Would Josh be able to care for his sister? What are you worried about, old woman? Just look at the two of them, she thought as she folded the dish towel and put it away.

Moma watched as Josh wiped the kitchen table clean and started folding the papers. After putting all the papers in their individual plastic sleeves, he placed them in a neat pile in a canvas bag. He worked quickly, doing six papers for each of his sister's one. He was as speedy as Angie was slow, but she didn't seem to mind that he was faster. *Nope, I have nothing to worry about*, thought Moma as she watched them working together.

Josh carried the heavy canvas bag through the room as the younger girl tried to help by hanging onto the sack. Angie's help actually slowed Josh down. He laughed as she almost pulled him backward with her dawdling pace. Her giggles filled the room as she tried to keep up with him.

Moma sipped her cup of tea as she observed the children through the front window. Josh carefully placed all the papers in the front basket of Angie's bike. He made sure she zipped up her coat; it was too warm for her hat and gloves. Taking off on her bike with a big smile, she was on her way, pumping the pedals as fast as she could, and never looking back.

Moma suddenly felt remiss. *I should have given her a kiss goodbye.* It was a strange thought for her. She was rarely physically demonstrative. *Silly old woman,* she thought, *I'll just give her a hug and kiss tonight.*

Two

But the serpent said to the woman: 'You certainly will not die! No, God knows well that the moment you eat of it, your eyes will be opened, and you will be like gods who know what is good and what is bad." (Gen. 3:5)

Evil is seldom quiet. It announces itself as it enters a room. Still, we refuse to see what is right in front of us. We think we can't stand to look at darkness because our hearts were made in the image of God, who is all-good. However, it is more likely we ignore evil because recognition requires a response. Worse, we tolerate much evil as long as it is attacking another; just happy it is leaving us alone. This is how the Father of Lies operates. He need not hide or blind us. In self-interest, we apply the blinders ourselves.

Tommy Ellis lay with his eyes open, but made no movement to get out of bed. He hated Saturdays. It wasn't that he loved school. He just hated being at home more. Here, there was no escape from the burning rage, the fury that threatened to consume his life. He could hear the rustling of the family downstairs and knew these stolen moments of peace would soon be over.

Still, Tommy wondered if the price he would pay for staying in bed, even for a few minutes, was worth the anger it would generate. He didn't know if it mattered anyway. He thought of Joe's rage as an ever-burning blue flame, quickly growing from red to white hot at the sight of Tommy's face. It didn't matter what the boy was doing at the time.

During the first few months of Joe's stay, Tommy had only seen glimpses of the burning hatred. It revealed itself in short smacks on the back of his head when his mother wasn't in the room and the cold stare of Joe's black eyes as he whispered what awaited Tommy if he ever complained to his mother.

Tommy was afraid. For a long time he didn't tell his mother. However, when Tommy turned five and the moments of anger grew in frequency and intensity, he did go to her. He thought she would protect him. Surely, he thought she would throw this monster of a boyfriend out of the house. The small boy dreamed of returning to the wonderful life he had before Joe wormed his way into their home.

His mother was alone in the basement, doing the laundry when, with a burst of courage and confidence, he climbed down the stairs to talk to her.

"Mommy," Tommy started, "Joe has been very mean to me." Tommy lifted the front of his shirt to show his mother the bruises.

His mother turned from her work and stared. Her face went white when she saw the numerous contusions across the tiny boy's chest and arms. It was a roadmap of abuse in various stages of healing.

"Please, Mommy," cried the five-year-old. "Please make Joe go away. He's so mean. He hits me when you're not around. Please send him away."

Tommy watched his mother's face as the emotions played across the blank screen of her eyes. He expected to see anger and was happy when her complexion turned from shocked white to an emotional red, sure he had done the right thing. *His mommy was angry the man was hitting him.* It wasn't until his mother reached over and grabbed his thin arm with force that he realized he had made the worse mistake of his life.

"What's wrong with you?" his mother hissed behind clenched teeth. "Don't you know how to keep your mouth shut? Let's go upstairs and ask Joe why he had to punish you. I'm sure he had a good reason."

"No . . . no!" screamed the boy as he felt his heart pounding in his chest. He pulled as hard as he could in an attempt to break away from his mother. His frail, 40-pound body was no match for the strength of her anger as she dragged him across the basement floor.

As they neared the bottom of the stairs, Tommy's fear reached its peak. He felt like a trapped animal and begged his mother for mercy. "Please don't tell Joe. Please . . . Mommy! I'll try to be a good boy. Please don't tell Joe."

He couldn't stop the flow of tears gushing from his eyes. Tommy felt nauseous as his stomach churned with terror. His mother didn't seem to notice as she dragged him up the basement stairs. He clung to the wooden stair rail. It slowed, but did not stop his ascent. As his mother pushed the basement door open and headed toward the kitchen and her boyfriend, the boy felt his head spin dizzily with deep, primal fear. He knew any hope he had for a safe life was about to end. Joe warned him what would happen if he complained to his mother. *Tommy knew he was about to die.*

In a sense, he did die that day. The loving, kind, and trusting part of his personality just curled up in a ball. Tommy swallowed his soul. It was as if he no longer existed. His mother tossed him hard, shaking, and hysterical, at the feet of his worst fear – the man who would make the rest of his life a misery.

Unable to hide his delight, Joe had trouble keeping the look of triumph off his face. "What's this about, Shirley? Why is the boy so upset?"

"He came to me with a story. He says you've been mean to him. He thinks you hate him," the bottle-blonde snickered.

"Oh, Shirley, you know the truth. You told me how much he reminds you of his sniveling father. He looks just like his old man, but what's worse, he acts just like him. Look at him groveling and whining. Is that any way for a man to act? Stand up, boy! I may be rough, but I'm going to make a man out of you"

Tommy was too frightened to move.

"Get up, you whining baby!" Joe shouted triumphantly as he lifted the boy roughly, dislocating his tiny shoulder.

The child's scream of pain only enraged Joe more. Yanking at the Tommy's arm, Joe threw him against the wall. The boy slid to the floor in silence. Tommy's mother picked him up and shoved him roughly onto a kitchen chair.

"See what you've done. You've upset Joe. You have to learn not to cause so much trouble. Be a good boy. Joe wants to be a father to you. He's going to teach you to be a man. You don't want to be like your bum of a father. He deserted us. He ran away without a thought of how we were going to live. Joe's going to marry me and be your father so you might as well learn to get along. Just obey him. We're going to be a family." Shirley looked for approval from Joe as she finished her tirade.

"Yes," the man's grin widened as he watched Shirley take his part, "we weren't going to tell you yet, but you might as well know. You're not going to be the only child. Your mother and I are expecting a baby. You'll learn that you're not the center of the earth when your new brother or sister arrives!"

Tommy sat in silence as Joe's face glowed with a sense of victory. The child knew he had lost. Things would only get worse. His shoulder throbbed with pain. He tried to move it, but it wouldn't budge. His mom noticed. Taking his arm in her hand, she moved it around and watched the child moan in pain.

"Oh, God, Joe, I think his arm is broken," she announced with fear.

For the first time, Tommy saw a look of concern wash over Joe's face. The man wasn't worried about Tommy. He hated the boy. Even at five, Tommy knew it was fear about being found out.

Joe walked over and yanked the arm roughly. Tommy could hear their voices, but couldn't make out the words, as the world turned grey and then black. The boy was consumed by the pain and his mind protected him by drawing him into the dark of unconsciousness.

When he awoke, he was in Joe's car, lying alone in the back seat. His mother turned and announced, "He's coming to, Joe." Tommy could feel the car pulling over to the side of the road. Joe opened the back seat door. Normally he would cringe in fear, but he was too numb to feel anything.

Joe's face grew red with rage as he bent into the back and shook his fist at the cringing boy. "Remember, you're clumsy. You fell down the basement stairs even though I told you repeatedly to stay away from the basement door. That's what you tell the doctor. And tell the same story to the nurses. You'll be sorry if you don't." He went back behind the wheel and drove the rest of the way to the emergency room.

Tommy did as he was told. The Doctor was suspicious but the boy insisted the story of falling down the basement stairs was true. It was the first of many ER visits and still more lies. He had reached out for help once. He would never make the same mistake again. That had been five years ago. His mom delivered twin sisters a few months later. They had the dark eyes and swarthy complexion of their father, and Joe adored them. Tommy wanted to hate them, but he couldn't. They were his little sisters, after all.

It was a strange thing, when Tommy did something wrong, Joe beat him. When the twins did something wrong, Joe got angry and beat Tommy. At first, he tried to defend himself, but later he took the beatings. He didn't want his little sisters to be crushed beneath Joe's anger.

Once in Sunday school, he learned the meaning of the word "scapegoat" and suddenly he realized his role in the family. Tommy was the scapegoat and his acceptance of the role saved everyone else. It didn't make it easier; it just made it simpler to understand. He knew it didn't matter what he did. If he was good, he was punched. If he was bad, he was punched harder.

Tommy knew it was really his fault after all. He was weak and the weak had to toughen up. He was just like his old man, a loser. Weak losers deserved what happened to them. He could hear his stepfather on the staircase. Tommy leaped out of bed and started to dress. *Perhaps Joe would just yell this time.* There was always that hope.

Joe was in a foul mood. His whole body shook with the anger and hatred he held for his stepson. With force, he pushed open the bedroom door.

As the door hit the wall, Joe shouted, "I'm sick of your lazy ways! You're just like your father – a no good bum."

The punches to the boy's chest were hard, but they had been harder in the past. Tommy bit his lip. Stoic, he kept his face still. He had learned not to show weakness. He bore the pain. Joe quickly decreed the punishment. First, Tommy would do without breakfast. Next, he would spend the morning raking the lawn. It was to be another dismal day.

Tommy dressed in his long-sleeved shirt. It covered the red marks. For hours, he raked the dormant grass of clinging leaves and broken branches. The leaves were unwilling to move from their cold, brown bed and the rake made scraping sounds against the half-frozen ground.

Three dark spirits watched Tommy from the peak of the roof. As Tommy's anger grew, the two smaller demons flapped their leathery wings in glee. The two spirits could hardly hold their enthusiasm in check and sought direction from the larger devil, the Spirit of Anger.

"Easy! Easy!" whispered the Spirit of Rage to himself as his red eyes glowed.

The Spirit of Murder clapped his claws. Still they waited. The Lead Spirit had not given the signal. It was so hard to remain, pulsating with anticipation; however, they knew the price of disobedience. Drugged with passion, they looked to the lead Spirit for the signal to swoop. Twice the size of the other devils, he finally raised his arm and pointed to the boy. The Spirit of Anger screamed with delight as he sent his minions. Their evil screams filled the air as they dove from the roof.

In the backyard, Tommy finally reached the last portion that needed raking, down by the crabapple tree. Then he saw the nest. He heard the baby birds crying for their mother. They were so hungry, so weak, and so dependent. Tommy took the nest off the tree branch. The two little, featherless birds continued to peep for their mother as he set the nest down on the grass.

He didn't see the spirits clinging to him, the demons that had flown from the roof to encourage him. The three devils whispered evil in the young boy's ears. Unaware of the demonic presence, Tommy picked up the old shovel that lay against the gnarled tree. With a good swing, he beat the little birds, crushing them to death. He knew it was the right thing to do; weak things didn't deserve to live.

Three

Light is sweet! And it is pleasant for the eyes to see the sun. However many years a man may live, let him, as he enjoys them all, remember that the days of darkness will be many. All that is to come is vanity. (Ecc. 10:7-8)

We doze in our beds unaware of the world that carries on as we dream: the shadow people who keep the world on simmer. As you turn over, the nurse checks on your grandmother in the retirement home and the security guard walks through the deserted mall. They are the twilight people who, like the cop who drives past your unlit home and the supermarket man who stocks the shelves, work unseen. On the graveyard shift, like markers in a book, they hold our place. We arise safely because they watched the moon and opened another day for us. Invisible, they melt away behind drawn blinds that block the sun, resting while we dance in the light.

Angie knew such a person. She was going to see him next. Pedaling quickly, she felt her heart beating faster. She was so worried about being late. The bakery was just half a block up, but still Angie hurried. Her next customer worked in the dark night and left early to sleep during the day.

When she first met him, Angie was afraid of Harold. She had

seen the vampire movies Josh loved. Whenever her brother turned the movies on, Angie would try to watch with him, but she was too afraid. Whenever the vampire went to bite the victim's neck, to drink her blood, she would hide her head in the sofa cushions.

The last time, Josh jumped up and pretended he was a vampire trying to bite Angie's neck. She screamed and rolled onto the floor to get away, but ended up being tickled by her older brother. Still, even though she did hide her eyes, Angie knew plenty about vampires. She knew garlic made them sick and that vampires slept during the day and stayed awake all night.

That's why – when she first met Harold – Angie was sure he was a vampire. She couldn't avoid delivering the paper to the bakery. If she evaded him, he might guess she suspected him and then she would be in real danger. She was sure anyone who worked all night and slept all day must be one of the living dead. The problem was she didn't know how she was going to prove it? She had to get help and no one would believe a little girl without proof. Anyway, everyone knew vampires could use their laser eyes to hypnotize adults.

No, Angie decided, *I need surprise vampire.* She carried some holy water from the font in the church to protect herself that morning. She ran up quickly and threw the holy water on the suspected fiend as he sat on the crate in the back of the bakery.

"What the . . .," the baker screamed as he felt the spray on his back. Jumping up in surprise, he turned.

Angie could feel her knees shake as the vampire started toward her. She knew she had to act quickly before he got a chance to use his laser vision. Lifting the bottle high in the air, she lowered her arm, dousing the front of the baker's white smock.

"Take that, you vampire!" she screamed. Angie hoped to see the parasite melt. Nothing happened. The man just stood there staring. Then he started to laugh. Angie's vision blurred and she almost blacked out from fear. She was sure the vampire would drink her blood. She hoped she would just die and go to Jesus. She didn't want to become one of the living dead. Everyone knew vampires liked to make little vampire slaves. Angie would hate that.

The baker didn't move toward her. Once he stopped laughing, he spoke in a mellow voice, "What makes you think I'm a vampire?"

Angie didn't know if she should talk to such an evil entity, but answered, "You up night, hide all day. You living dead."

"If I were a vampire, wouldn't the holy water burn me?"

She was confused. "It make vampire melt."

"Throw it on me again. That will prove I'm not a vampire."

He allowed her to sprinkle him again with the holy water. When Angie threw the water on Harold, he didn't smoke up and burn as the vampires did on TV. Angie was relieved. She knew any real vampire would have melted.

After the holy water incident, Harold and Angie became great friends. Harold waited for Angie on Saturdays. He gave her the day-old bread and rolls, coffee cakes, and buns that used to be thrown out. Angie would bring the still tasty treats to the poor side of town and deliver them with the paper to everyone's delight. Today she was troubled. She had started late. *Oh, please, Jesus, please have Harold be there*, she prayed quietly as she pedaled her bike too fast. She would miss all the gifts if she were too late for Harold.

Turning into the parking lot of the small, stucco bakery, Angie was thrilled to see Harold sitting on a crate by the back door. "He waited for me," she cried with happiness. Skidding to a quick stop, she almost went into the wall of the bakery, and barely missed falling off her bike.

"Whoa! Easy there, Angie! You'll get hurt if you don't slow down." Harold held his hands in the air and smiled.

"Sorry, me so late." She blushed with anxiety.

"Don't worry. I wouldn't go home without seeing you. I'd always wait for my friend." The plump man rubbed the middle of his head, which was completely bald. His large hands were white with flour.

Angie was fascinated with Harold's hairless head. There was only hair on the sides and on the lower back of his head. Angie's teacher was constantly saying that teaching the kids in her special class was like pulling her hair out. Angie remembered asking the baker if he pulled out his hair in frustration. Again, Harold laughed for a long time. He liked to laugh. It was one of the reasons she liked him so. Moma said to stay away from people who never smiled. Like that old crab face down the block, she thought as she smiled at Harold.

"Thanks you wait. Lots deliveries today," Angie answered.

"Well, today is your lucky day. I have plenty of leftover breads and rolls. And guess what? I also have extra sweet buns and coffee cakes."

Harold was pleased to help Angie bundle the breads and the rolls in the rear holders on her bike. Angie reached into the plastic bag that held the sweet buns and day-old coffee cakes and removed three sweet buns. She placed them in the waxed-paper bag in the front basket of her bike.

"Angie, why are you taking three buns to Mrs. Hansen's house?" Harold asked with curiosity, "You usually only take two, one for her and one for you."

The girl paused to form her thoughts. "She very sour. Moma say she just old sourpuss. Extra sweet roll be help maybe."

All set, she pulled out one of the papers and gave it to Harold.

"Here you paper," Angie said. "What you do now, sleep?"

"Oh, I guess I'll just go home and read the paper with my tea. Hopefully, I'll get tired and go to sleep."

Angie could see the pain on Harold's face as he thought about the day ahead of him.

"Why you sad?" she asked with compassion.

"Oh, it's nothing really. I guess I just miss Edna. Life seems so pointless without her."

Angie could see the faraway look in Harold's eyes as he thought of his deceased wife. She knew it had been ten years, all of Angie's life, since Edna died. .

"Why you sad? She be in heaven," she stated.

"I guess you're right, Angie, but, I feel so lonely since Edna died.

My life is just an endless cycle of work and sleep. Life is so lonely without someone to share it with." The plump man sighed. "Every day I go home to empty rooms. I have no one to talk to. I listen to the TV and the radio just to hear a human voice."

Angie thought hard. She tried to imagine what it would be like to go home and not have Moma and Josh there. She couldn't make her mind think it.

"You need new wife. Go marry one." She smiled, satisfied at her simple solution.

Harold laughed. "I'll never marry again. Edna was the only girl for me. Besides whom would I marry? I don't even have a girlfriend."

Angie seemed puzzled as she looked at her friend, "You no old like Moma. Many years alone you be."

His eyes darkened. Again, he sighed staring ahead as if he were looking out over the long empty years ahead. "Well, I guess I'll just have to get used to being alone. Hey, who would want to marry a bald baker who sleeps during the day?" Harold patted Angie's head with affection, "I don't know Angie, do you think Moma would have me?"

Angie looked puzzled at the question. "Oh, no, Moma too old. She be dead long before you. You need someone else."

Harold looked at the girl. She couldn't possibly understand the problems of adults. He couldn't understand why he was even burdening this child with his worries.

Wanting to make the conversation more lighthearted, Harold laughed. "That's just it, Angie, there is no one else, no one else for me. It's okay though. I had the love of my life. No one could be like Edna. I could never marry someone like Edna again."

Angie looked angry, "Of course not, no marry Edna. She dead. 'Cause you more dead than her."

He was stunned. "What do you mean? I'm not dead!"

Angie stood her ground. "You more dead than Edna. She be in

heaven. She happy. You the dead one. No life for you."

Harold could sense all the pain and loneliness rising up from his broken heart. He tried to push it down again, but the words of this child pierced his soul. He tried not to think about the night Edna died. Now it all came flooding back, suffocating him. For eight months the cancer had eaten away at her body until she became the ghost of the woman he loved. Edna, the Edna he knew and loved ceased to exist. In her place was a skeleton with vacant eyes that seemed to look beyond the veil. The only part of this world that remained with his wife was the pain that riddled her body, causing it to stiffen in agony long before the next pain shot was due.

Her husband was well aware of each pain shot for he was the one who had given Edna those injections. She should have been in a nurse's care. In a hospice, they might have made her more comfortable, but Harold had promised her that he would keep her at home. She could die in her own bed. They lived in rooms above his bakery and he would bake through the night, while keeping an eye on Edna. The morning she died, he was so tired.

It had been eight months of less than two full hours sleep at a time. It seemed like an eternity of changing diapers and trying to force food. It felt longer than a lifetime of pulling at tight flesh so the needles would not hit the prominent bones of her emaciated body.

Harold's muscles ached from lack of sleep. His eyes burned red with weariness. Endless days of watching the woman who was his life wither away had taken its toll. His head was pounding. He heard her stirring in the other room, the moaning and whining that wouldn't stop until another pain shot was given. It was two more hours before the next shot was due. He couldn't face another sleepless day. He pounded on the table.

"Take her! Let her die already! Let me sleep," he cried as he laid his head down on the arm that was lying on the table. Harold didn't remember anything else. When he awoke, the afternoon sun had spanned the sky. The apartment was quiet. He could hear the bustle of the bakery below, but there was no sound from the bedroom.

Rushing to Edna's bedside, he knew before he even saw her. She had stopped breathing. Unable to move, he heard screaming. It wasn't until the girls from the bakery ran up the stairs that Harold realized it was his scream.

It was his fault. He had prayed for her death. He had wished her dead before he fell asleep. His heart broke knowing his selfishness had caused her death. *How could God ever forgive him? How could he ever forgive himself?* He had killed her. It was he who deserved to die.

Had she cried in pain while he was in an unconscious slumber? Harold would never know. He didn't deserve her love. He didn't deserve any love. His loneliness was a just punishment for what he had wished. Turning from Angie, Harold covered his face with his hands and sobbed deeply. He wanted to stop but couldn't. He didn't want to frighten the child. When he had finally regained control, he looked up expecting to see Angie had left. Instead, she stood quietly by.

"I'm sorry, I didn't mean to cry like that." Harold tried to dismiss his pain.

"No be sorry. Most you be alive in long time," the small girl answered. "You so alone, no live, just work. No really happy, just pretend."

He didn't want to talk about his feelings. It was too painful. Turning to Angie, he said, "You're just a little girl. You don't understand how adults are. Just leave me alone."

Angie's face flushed with emotion.

Not able to express her thoughts, she yelled, "No try to go back to dead again."

Harold tried to calm the child. "You're so young. You just don't understand about such things."

Angie pulled away, her face contorted in rage. Running to her bike, she bent and untied the bag that held the day-old bread. Taking a large loaf of rye from the bag, Angie threw it on the sidewalk. Jumping as high in the air as she could, she came down with both feet on the loaf of bread breaking it in half. Then jumping alternately with both feet, she crushed the bread to crumbs.

Harold was frightened by the child's behavior. Clearly, she was beside herself. *What have I done?* he thought as he rushed over to her. Reaching out and grabbing her shoulders, he tried to calm the child.

"Angie, what are you doing? Why are you destroying the bread I gave you?" He tried to use a soothing voice to settle the overwrought child.

"Why not? I break gift from you. Just like you break gift from God. How it feel?" She sniffled as she tried to speak through her emotions.

Harold was in shock and asked in rapid fire," What do you mean? What have I broken? What gift have I received from God?"

Angie took a deep breath and tried to calm herself with little success. "You throw away days, weeks, years. Life gift. You throw away."

Harold fell back as the truth of what the child was saying struck him. "You don't understand. You don't feel my pain. You don't understand what was between Edna and me."

Angie stopped crying, but stamped her foot in anger. "No! Edna not happy. You stomp gift. You waste!"

The man took the child in his arms. He could feel her tiny body quiver with emotion. A strange feeling came over him. His thoughts had been murky for so long and now he felt as if a cloud was lifting. His mind grew sharp. He felt his life force revive and wondered how long he'd been asleep.

Pulling back, he looked with new eyes at the child before him. *Who would have thought this handicapped mind could hold such simple wisdom?*

Wiping the tears from her eyes, Harold wanted to comfort her. "Angie, you're right. I have been dead for the last ten years. I've been so lost in the pain and grief of losing Edna, that I've been living my life by remote control. I refused to feel the pain because it seemed too much for me. I resigned myself to a life of lonely emptiness."

Looking at Angie, Harold chuckled. The quizzical child had

not understood a word he just said. He quickly decided to make it simple. "You are right. I should find a new wife, but who would marry me? Edna and I weren't blessed with children, so who would help me or want me?"

Subdued now, Angie smiled. "I know. You marry Ruthie."

Harold grinned, happy to see the child was calm now. "Ruthie? Who's Ruthie?"

Angie smiled wider. "Oh Ruthie work at diner. She have four kids, no husband. She very pretty, but with no make-up she look old like you."

The baker laughed at the child's enthusiasm. "Well, thanks for the tip. I guess I'll look Ruthie up."

"Okay then. Gotta go," Angie announced as she sat on her bike and started to ride. Heading away, she turned and waved to her friend. Her troubles seemed so easily forgotten.

Harold chuckled at the child. She recovered so quickly. Besides, it was such a silly idea. Getting in his old Ford truck, he started down Main Street. He couldn't stay in the apartment above the bakery after Edna died. It was too full of memories. He had bought a modest ranch on the outskirts of town. It was such a ridiculous thought. He laughed. Imagine him dating again. However, as he passed the diner, he turned his head to take a quick look.

Four

My God, my God, why have you abandoned me? Why so far from my call for help, from my cries of anguish? My God, I call by day, but you do not answer; by night, but I have no relief. (Psalm 22: 1-2)

Homes usually reflect their owners. Are they simple or ornate, overly neat or messy? An overly neat home is indicative of the owner's need to be perfect, or at least perfect in the eyes of others. Messy, yet clean homes mirror free spirits too busy living to take the time to straighten up. A dirty home is frequently evidence of depression, the home shouting how little the owners think of themselves.

Mrs. Inga Hansen's home was a Victorian, laden with the gingerbread touches of the period. The freshly painted porch spanned the entire front of the home and hirelings watered the bowls of purple inpatients that hung flawlessly from the porch roof. The porch swing possessed no scrape marks in its shadow.

Angie parked her bike in front and carried the bag of sweet buns and the paper through the yard to the kitchen door. Knocking lightly, she entered to her awaiting customer. Mrs. Hansen, who had seen Angie's arrival, was pouring tall glasses of milk and preparing for the weekly snack with Angie. When Angie pulled out the three buns, the tall, red-haired woman placed them on the table.

"Why three buns? Are you hungry today?" asked Mrs. Hansen, her face pinched in disapproval.

"Oh no! Two buns you. I eat one," answered Angie as she sat in her customary chair.

"And just why would I eat two? Do you want me to get fat?" Mrs. Hansen asked harshly.

"Oh, you so sour, like a squeezed up, old lemon. Always, but worse sour last week. Two buns help maybe?" Angie reached for her bun, anxious to enjoy the treat. She didn't look up as she dunked the edge of the bun in the milk and dripped some on the table before taking a bite. Angie didn't see the anger building in the woman who sat across from her. Finally looking up, she sensed the annoyance that drove Mrs. Hansen to speak.

"You little brat! Is this the thanks I get for being kind to you? You have some nerve talking to your elders that way. Say you're sorry or get out of my house right now!"

Angie didn't seem flustered. "Me no sorry, Me truth. You no like, but still truth."

Mrs. Hansen's mouth puckered in distain. "Who are you to talk to me like that, you dumb-dumb!"

Angie laughed. "You may think that I am dumb, but it is God that I come from!"

A sense of pride filled the young girl as she remembered the poem.

Mrs. Hansen blushed with irritation. "And who taught you that little piece of nonsense?"

Putting her bun back on her plate, Angie answered, "It no nons . . .Moma teach me!"

Clearly trying to control herself, Mrs. Hansen snapped, "It is nonsense and your grandmother shouldn't' be teaching you such lies. There is no God and you're wasting your time to believe there is."

"I no believe – I know. What wrong you, no believe God?" Angie asked with concern.

"Just look around you. Look at the people in this world. Look at the pain and suffering. Look at how horrible people are. Just look at how horrible people are to you. What kind of God would create such a world?" The older woman was shocked at her own intensity.

Angie took another bite of her bun and spoke with her mouth full. "No ask world, world know God. Ask you. Why you so sour? World good, you old sour lemon, eat sweet bun!"

"Oh, do you think a stupid sweet bun can make me happy. What made me happy is gone and will never come back again. No sweet bun is going to help that." The older woman pursed her lips.

Angie was not deterred, "You so sour and hard on outside, but good and soft on inside. You all alone, sit in house, no friend but Angie. Why you hide in house?"

Mrs. Hansen took a sip of her milk. Angie watched as the woman tried to steady herself.

"I don't want any friends. You're my friend and I don't need any other friends. I have no reason to go out of the house. There's nothing out there for me. Everything I love is right here. I'm going to stay here until I die."

Angie squinted and looked around at the kitchen. "Who you love here? Nobody here."

Mrs. Hansen took another sip of milk. She already regretted the way she had talked to the child. It wasn't the child's fault. *Angie was so simple, how could she understand the true way of life.* The bitter woman decided to act with more kindness.

Mrs. Hansen's wrinkled face puckered to hold the pain within. "He used to sit on the floor, right there by the sink, banging on the pots with a wooden spoon. It used to irritate me because of all the expensive toys he ignored."

"Who play pots?" Angie asked.

Mrs. Hansen stared at the girl. "I can't believe that you're asking me that. You know who I'm talking about."

The girl looked up from her treat. "No, no know."

Mrs. Hansen rose, her face wizened with emotion, and took the girl by the hand. "Come with me and I'll show you who I'm talking about."

Angie shoved the last big piece of cake into her mouth and, with both cheeks puffed out, allowed herself to be lead into the parlor. The living room was large and dark. Heavy, brown furniture filled the room, matching the dark panels of wainscot that lined the walls. A satin paper of gold and red covered the upper wall, but didn't lighten the burdensome room.

The woman watched as Angie wrinkled her nose. The room smelled of lemon oil teased with mold. Despite the fire that blazed in the ornate fireplace, the room felt damp and cold.

Releasing Angie's hand, Mrs. Hansen pointed to the oil painting above the mantle. "That's him, that's my boy."

Angie took a good look at the oversized painting, framed in ornate gold. A young man sat looking out at something unknown. His suit was perfect as were the hands folded in his lap. His eyes looked so empty and his face seemed cold as if this was the last place he wanted to be.

"I had this painting done at the beginning of his senior year. It is a perfect rendering of Karl."

"Me hope not. He look so sad in eyes," answered Angie as she swallowed the dry lump of cake in her mouth.

The tall woman looked up at the portrait again with concern. "Why yes, I remember that day. He didn't want to sit for the artist. He wanted to be out with his friends. I begged him to be patient, but he was always so restless. You're too young to remember Karl."

With her mouth free of food, Angie answered, "Oh, me know dead boy. Boy die on prom night, killed by drunk in car. Everyone in town know dead Karl. Talk about him walking by house – house like graveyard. Look at house and talk dead Karl. Like graveyard house. Karl all dead and mother buried in house, too."

Inga Hansen felt her heart beat harder as tears formed in her eyes. In a soft voice, she answered, "That's not true. How can you say such a thing? People don't say that. People remember Karl. He had such a great, open, and loving personality."

Angie shook her head. "Nope, it truth. Dead Karl and sad, crazy mother all people say."

"That's ridiculous! Karl was full of life. Everyone loved him. When he walked into a room, it filled with light. He brought joy and laughter everywhere he went. Everyone must remember how special he was." Tears fell softly from her eyes.

"Nope, no one remember live Karl – only dead Karl and lock-up mother. Me know dead Karl and sad prom night. No know any laughing Karl."

Inga was stunned, not angry. "Look, here are more pictures of Karl."

She opened a photo album that had been lying on the coffee table. Sitting on the couch, she waved her hand indicating that Angie should sit beside her. "Look, here's Karl skiing. He loved to ski. Oh, and over here he's playing baseball. He loved sports. It was hard to keep up with him. He had such a zest for life."

Angie looked at the smiling face in the photos. "He look so happy."

Mrs. Hansen brightened as she turned the page of the album. "He was always happy, always telling jokes. He could remember the punch lines, unlike his mother. I don't ever remember being in a room with Karl where there wasn't laughter."

Mrs. Hansen sighed, thinking of the joy that Karl always felt. He was the opposite of her father. She had been raised on a farm. Her father was a distant man, cold and silent. Inga loved her lively and social mother, who had died when Inga was eleven. Having no siblings, she looked desperately for her father's approval. She remembered bringing him her report card. She was beaming with pride over the high grades. He slowly took his reading glasses out of his pocket and looked, without even a smile.

"School is okay and it would matter if you were a boy. A girl doesn't need an education. Learning how to clean and cook is the thing," he answered tossing her report card down on the table. Inga could feel her heart break as he left her standing alone in the kitchen, without a word.

She did learn to cook and clean. Each day she went to school and came home to clean the house and cook her father's dinner. At first, she had difficulty with no one to teach her how to cook. Her father would toss her attempts right into the trash without a word.

Inga got some cookbooks and, after some experimenting, she noticed that her father cleaned his plate. He never said a word about the food. Inga washed the laundry and ironed his shirts and handkerchiefs without a response from him. She noticed he threw his dirty clothes in the laundry, but never commented on the care she took.

Inga worked for years trying to win his approval. His silence was like a suffocating, dark blanket that covered her soul. When she won the lead in the school play, she was so excited that she burst into his study. Inga was so eager to announce her news, she failed to notice the anger on his face.

"Papa, I won the lead in the play. The teacher said I was a natural talent. I even get to sing. She said I had a soprano voice that was as clear as a bell. Will you come and see me in the play?" she asked.

Looking over his newspaper, her father snapped, "This is your excuse for your rudeness? Did you think it was all right to fly into my room without knocking? You're supposed to be a lady. Your mother was a lady. I don't know where you learned your behavior, but it is unacceptable."

For once Inga was too happy to let his coldness deter her, "But will you come Papa? I would like you to hear me sing."

Her father lifted the paper up to continue reading. She couldn't see his face as he answered. "I have no time to waste on such nonsense and neither do you. Tomorrow you will tell that stupid teacher that you have too much work at home to be done. You have no time for a silly play."

He rattled the newspaper, his way of letting her know that the discussion was over. It was as if she was seeing him for the first time and she felt hatred for him. Inga had always thought that if she was good enough, or pretty enough, or even smart enough, she would win his love. Now she knew she would never get love from him. He had no love to give.

When she left the study that day and closed the door, she also closed her heart to him. She was obedient and quit the play, much to the teacher's disappointment. Inga's chest burned and she suppressed the sobs rising from her spirit as she watched another girl play her part. She watched as the girl's father handed his daughter a large bouquet of roses. It was the end. She never looked for love from her father again.

She turned to other men. She was tall and attractive and had no problems attracting the boys in her class. There was a special boy. His blond hair and green eyes decorated her dreams. Marty's father owned a small farm just on the edge of town. His large family barely subsisted on the meager wages his father earned at the local grocery store. The sons worked the farm, which supplemented the family's diet. She spent most of her senior year with Marty, a time full of dreams of marriage and an escape from the emptiness of her life.

Right after graduation, she secured a job down at the local bank although she still cooked and cleaned for her father. Marty had won a scholarship and would be leaving for college in August. As the summer days dwindled and the nights began to cool, Inga's fear of being alone gripped her. He was to leave within the week and she was so afraid. Her fear guided her right into his bed. They spent the last week making love.

She was happy. Secure in his love, she watched as the train carried him away to his dream of a degree. They both knew that unless he made something of himself, her father would never allow the marriage. Inga returned to her routine until the fall brought cold wind and fallen leaves. It also brought the frightened girl the realization that she was having Marty's child.

There was no one for her to turn to and she never even considered going to her father for help. What transpired seemed ordained as fear guided her decisions. Karl Hansen was the manager of the bank, a widower who had his eye on the pretty, young girl in the outer office. Inga had ignored his flirting, but now without much thought, she responded. Within a week of her returned attention, she was out with the 60-year-old man. He was 15 years older than her father. Within two weeks she gave in to his desire. It was easy to convince Karl Hansen that the baby was his. Her father wouldn't come to the wedding. He told her she was a disgrace and that he never wanted to see her or the baby. Inga moved from the home of one cold man into another.

Karl Hansen's home was a dilapidated Victorian in the next town. Inga was excited. She dreamed of painting and decorating. The home was large and roomy, but her new husband was too cheap to spend any money to update it. He made her life miserable, pinching every penny. He accused her of tricking him into marriage for his money. The partial truth of his accusation hardened her.

After his death, three years into their marriage, she discovered the large amount of money he had hidden. After redoing the home, she turned all her love to her son.

Marty graduated with an accounting degree and arrived at her front door after his return home from college. He looked at the young babe in the playpen on the porch and recognized his own mother's eyes. Inga denied it. She had grown cold, afraid he was just after her money. Most of her fear was because of her son. She watched with mixed feelings as Marty left. He never returned to see his son again. Inga finally had all of someone's love. She had no desire to share.

Inga Hansen sighed. The memories were so painful. She had told so many lies. She had taken a father from her son. *That was why God had taken her son from her.* She was sure of it. She was alone now. *Karl had died because of her sins.* She didn't have any doubt. Pulling herself away from her guilt, she turned her attention to the young girl.

Angie looked around. "No laugh here – dead room for dead boy. No Karl who laughs here."

Mrs. Hansen raised her head and looked around. "Yes, it does seem dead, dead like Karl. But what can I do? I can't bring him back."

Angie got up from her seat and walked over to the front window. It was covered by heavy tapestry draperies. Taking hold of the middle panel, she pulled the drapery to the side. "See now light, day come in, dark run away."

The bright sunlight penetrated the room, casting dust mites away from the window. Looking out, Angie saw the neighbor passing. "Hi Mrs. Lennon!" The startled woman almost dropped her grocery bag when she heard the voice coming from the solitary mansion.

Looking up and seeing Angie waving, she smiled and yelled, "Hello, Angie, will you be coming to my house with the paper?"

"Yeah, me be coming."

"Hello, Inga, it's so nice to see you."

Angie hadn't seen Mrs. Hansen rise from the couch and approach. Before she could comment, the angry woman pulled the window panel closed with such force that she almost ripped the drapes down.

Her breathing heavy with outrage, she snapped, "Who told you to touch my window? You keep your hands off of things that don't belong to you."

Angie's eyes had trouble adjusting to the dark again. "Why you no say hello Mrs. Lennon. She nice."

"Why wouldn't she be nice? She has five healthy children. They come and visit all the time. She has five and I have none." She nudged the girl out to the kitchen.

"Oh, so you want hers be dead like yours?" Angie tilted her head.

The woman pushed Angie out the door to the kitchen porch. "Get out of here and don't ever come back!"

Angie shook her head. "Better eat sweet bun, you badder than last week."

The back screen door slammed shut. "Get out! I don't need you.

Get out and don't come back."

Angie walked toward her bike and yelled as she kicked the bike stand up, "Better eat sweet bun, you old sour puss. See you next week."

Five

O, God, you are my God – for you I long! For you my body yearns; for you my soul thirsts, like a land parched, lifeless, and without water. (Psalm 63:2)

We are born with a hunger for love. That hunger drives us, leading us in so many directions. We try to fill the emptiness with friends or lovers. Often the need for love from other people leads us into sin, for we haven't learned to love ourselves. When people, who are only human, fail us, the pain becomes too much to bear. The emptiness becomes a deep wound that doesn't heal. Many of us try to numb the pain with alcohol, drugs, or even food. Others, who want a distraction from the pain, turn to work, or success, or money to fill the meaninglessness.

Turning to the things of the world will not heal the wounds. In time the disappointment hardens us, turning our hearts to stone. For we have lost our way. The only one who can fill the emptiness that was purposely placed within our infant hearts is God. It is all a journey, a journey home to the Source. Oh, the things of this world are good. They are here to teach us. He leads us gently. Teaching us to give and receive love – until we are ready to receive the greatest love of all, the love of our Creator.

Mrs. Lennon's home was as light as Mrs. Hansen's was dark. It was as filled with the noise of life as the other carried the silence of the tomb. Angie loved to visit with the small, stout woman who sang songs as she baked treats for her grandchildren. The woman's eyes would sparkle with welcome as Angie delivered the paper.

"Oh my, I wonder what's doing today. I love to read the paper with my tea. Come while I put the kettle on." Mrs. Lennon waved Angie into the bright kitchen in the back of the house.

"Why you like?" Angie asked as she handed the paper across the table.

"Well, I love the crossword puzzle although I am not always good at it. Sometimes I can't figure the words at all."

Angie thought hard. "Oh, like homework. Make Angie dizzy."

The grey-haired woman laughed. "Well, I guess you're right, I was never any good at homework either."

"What else you like?" Angie asked as she sat at the kitchen table.

"Well, I hate to say it, but I love the gossip." Mrs. Lennon smiled at her own failing. "You know, when the children were little, they were involved in all of the town's business. They played baseball and soccer. They knew everyone in school. I enjoyed hearing all the town happenings. I enjoyed being the first to know the latest news, such as who lost his job or who was getting a divorce. I was privy to the news of which politician was on the take or who was fooling around with whose wife."

"Kids no tell now?" asked Angie as she watched the woman fuss around the kitchen.

Bending to pull the latest tray of cookies from the oven, she answered, "No, the children are all grown up and gone, married with their own homes. My grandchildren go to schools in other towns. Nope, now I only get my news from the paper you bring each Saturday."

"Oh, cookies smell good," exclaimed Angie, licking her lips.

"Well, the baking sheet is too hot. Let me get you one. Anyway, Angie, what news do you hear in the school hallways?"

Angie took a bite of the warm, oatmeal-raisin cookie and mumbled, "No know. It hurt head to think fights, trouble. Moma say better ways use time."

Mrs. Lennon blushed. "What does your Moma mean?"

"Oh, she say better see what kids need and give, then talk what bad them," answered the girl as she tilted her head to listen to the strange sound coming from garage. "What that? What that crying?"

Blushing at the truth of Moma's take on gossip, Mrs. Lennon was glad of the distraction. "Finish the cookie and I'll show you."

Angie gobbled down the rest of the cookie and followed the woman to the garage door. When Mrs. Lennon opened the door, the excited girl ran into the garage, squealing with delight.

"Puppies! Where you get all puppies?"

Just inside the garage, Lady, Mrs. Lennon's golden retriever was lying on her pillow bed, with eight little puppies around her. Angie ran up to the noisy bunch and crawled right in the middle of the squirming fray. She rolled around and giggled as the puppies licked her face and tugged on her clothes.

"Where you get?" She laughed.

Giggling, Mrs. Lennon answered, "Lady is their mother. And they're all pedigree-golden retrievers."

"What you do? So many dogs!" Angie asked as she hugged a chubby pup.

"Oh, tomorrow they'll be eight weeks old. I'm going to put an ad in the paper. I should be able to get at least $500 a puppy."

Angie's eyes widened as she tried to count the puppies. "Wow! You be rich!"

Mrs. Lennon pulled the girl up from the squealing passel of fur. "Come on now, they have to rest with their mother. Puppies need a lot of sleep."

Angie reluctantly left the garage and entered the kitchen as the puppies tried to follow. Mrs. Lennon closed the door carefully. "I love the puppies, but now that they can run around, they keep me on my toes."

"Too bad you sell. Mrs. Hansen lonely – need puppy friend." Angie answered as she prepared to leave.

The stout woman smiled as what Angie said inspired her. "Here, Angie take another cookie with you. I don't know why I keep baking. With no children around, I end up throwing most of what I cook away. There's no one to eat it all."

"Me take one for Billy." Angie carefully wrapped a large, chocolate chip cookie in a paper napkin and placed it in her pocket. Looking at the three sheets of cookies on the counter, Angie was amazed. "No throw, lots kids, no Moma. You be Moma them."

"Who do you mean, Angie? Who needs a grandmother with lots of cookies?"

Angie jumped on her bike before she answered. "Kids at center. No cookies. No Moma. You go. Goodbye."

Angie turned her bike in the direction of the diner. She didn't see Mrs. Lennon's thoughtful look.

Returning to the garage, Mrs. Lennon picked up one of the female puppies and headed out to the backyard. Sneaking around the fence, she placed the pup at her neighbor's back door. Hidden behind the stockade fence, she watched through a small opening. As expected, the puppy started whining. It wasn't long before Mrs. Hansen opened the door to see where the fuss was coming from. Sternly staring down, she seemed stunned at the sight of the small animal. Stepping out on the porch, she looked around to see the owner, but didn't spot anyone. As she looked, the puppy started to lick her foot.

Reaching down, she picked up the friendly puppy and asked, "What are you doing here? How did you get here?" The pup licked her face in response.

Mrs. Lennon watched as her next-door neighbor smiled despite herself. She heard Inga say, "Well, I guess you can come in and have something to eat. But that doesn't mean you can stay. I don't have time for a dog."

The puppy responded with an excited yelp as if to put the lie to the lonely woman's words. Mrs. Lennon felt lighthearted as she returned to her kitchen and her now cold cup of tea. She looked at the tabloid on the table and thought about starting up the kettle for a leisurely read. Instead, she found herself placing the cookies in her carry-all tray. Maybe she should go down to the community center and see just what was going on.

Angie stopped at the curb. Josh had taught her to always cross the street at the light and to walk her bike across. Even though the light turned red and all the cars stopped, Angie looked both ways to make sure it was safe. She had to cross the street to get to the diner and the other customers on her route.

Angie mumbled as she waved her pointer finger at the car that almost went through the red light and screeched to a stop over the painted line.

"Hey you, watch step. Where you get license? At five-dime store?" She didn't really know what a five-and-dime store was. Angie had learned what to say to bad drivers from Josh, who had learned the expression from Moma. Safely across the street, she jumped back on her bike and headed toward the diner.

She counted twice to be sure she had the 15 papers that Ruthie, the blond waitress, wanted before going in.

"Hey, Angie, you're a little late today." Ruthie smiled as she placed a cup of coffee in front of the old man at the counter.

"Me very busy. Got papers here," answered Angie with her arms overloaded with her delivery.

Ruthie took the pile of papers and placed them by the register for the customers to take.

"Slow down and take a load off your feet."

Angie looked at her feet and wondered what load Ruthie was talking about. Sitting in the booth with Billy, she watched as he finished coloring a dinosaur with a green crayon.

"You good. Be real artist," Angie told the five-year-old.

Billy smiled. "I want to be an artist, but my sisters say it's a stupid thing to want. Artists are poor."

Angie looked shocked. "Oh no, if you be artist, it be in your heart. It means Daddy God put it there."

"What do you mean? Who's Daddy God and how did he put that in my heart?"

Angie scratched her head, trying to think of how to explain Daddy God.

"Daddy God make you. He make me and everybody."

"How did he make me?" Billy asked with curiosity. Angie rubbed her forehead. This was a hard question. She remembered her teacher saying something about clay, but that story seemed silly. Angie decided to tell Billy how she figured God made everybody.

"It like in doll factory." Angie struggled to explain her vision of creation to the wide-eyed boy.

"Boy dolls and girl dolls ride on factory belt, in and out of machines. Machines paint on eyes and hair. Dolls just lay, dead like toys. They get to end. In end, sits Daddy God in big chair. He pick up each boy, girl doll. He puff and breathe hard on doll."

"How do you know this?" asked Billy.

"Oh, Angie hear Father Hughes say. God breathing. Think out rest myself."

Billy nodded his head as if convinced of the truth of Angie's information. "Then what happens?"

"Oh, then Daddy God breathes hard on doll and doll gets new face. Face all own. Like no one else has. Doll starts breathe. Come alive."

"What does that have to do with me being a poor artist?" Billy asked.

"Quiet! I get that. When doll alive, Daddy takes finger. Points it right here," Angie said, indicating her chest. "He pokes hard – touches new heart. Poking put what new person 'sposed to be in heart. You have dreams what to be. Daddy God poked you there."

Billy said happily, "Good, then I will be a poor artist. What did Daddy God poke into you?"

Angie hesitated. "Me never think, me no grown-up ideas. Maybe Daddy God forgot poke Angie. Ask Father Hughes. He know everything."

Remembering her gift, Angie announced, "Me got surprise you."

Billy closed his coloring book and his eyes lit up. "What's the surprise?"

"Close eyes," Angie instructed, laughing as she watched Billy squirm in excitement. Pulling the chocolate chip cookie from her pocket, Angie giggled. "Okay."

Billy quickly popped the treat in his mouth as Ruthie brought Angie a glass of milk. Usually Ruthie stayed to talk to Angie for a few minutes, but today she seemed in a rush. She scurried over to the other side of the diner to talk to a thin, blond man who sipped coffee while he looked out the window.

"Busy today?" Angie asked Billy.

"No. Mommy likes that new man. He's her new boyfriend." Billy pouted.

Angie looked at the man. "He nice, no like?"

Billy shook his head negatively.

"Mom gets you Dad. You no want one?" Angie tilted her head.

Billy just sighed as Ruthie headed their way with a wide smile and a dreamy expression. Angie thought Ruthie would be prettier if she didn't have so much make-up and such puffy hair.

"That new boyfriend?" Angie asked.

"I hope so," answered the waitress as she looked longingly down the aisle. "Don't you think he's handsome?"

Angie stared at the man, who seemed oblivious to the people watching him. "No, look like last man."

"How can you say that?" exclaimed Ruthie. "My last boyfriend was dark and heavy. This man is blond and thin. They don't look alike at all."

"No, they same," declared Angie as she sipped her milk.

"How are they the same?" asked the exasperated waitress.

"Look. Jumping feet. Moma says feet know want to leave before man know."

Ruthie stared at the truck driver's feet. His brown-booted feet were tapping as his knees were pumping up and down. Her last boyfriend had the same habit, but she never made the connection.

"What else do you see that's the same?" Ruthie whispered.

"Go check eyes," answered Angie.

The girl gave no further clues and the waitress started down the aisle to see her prospective lover.

"Hi Tom, want me to top that coffee off?" asked the waitress with a seductive lilt in her voice.

Ruthie was pleased when his eyes met hers, sparkling with delight. Ruthie was sure this man was different, different from all the men who had lined her past with disappointment. There had been so many men who filled her heart with hope. Yet, one by one, they had entered her life for such short periods. Most of the men had left her with nothing. Four men had left her with a child who would never know the father who had been just passing through. Ruthie had hope for Tom. Maybe he would be different. Putting down the coffee pot, she slid onto the red-vinyl bench across the table from him.

Thinking of Angie's warning, she was delighted when his eyes glowed with interest as he returned her gaze. Ruthie felt encouraged. Perhaps this man would be different from the others. Perhaps this man would stay. However, as the 43-year-old hopefully watched Tom's face, she saw him lose interest in her small talk. His eyes looked out the window, staring at the open road in front of the diner. His feet shuffled as his knees pumped up and down.

Funny, she thought, I never noticed that faraway look in his eyes. And what's worse, I've seen that look in all the other men's eyes.

She remembered that look in her father's eyes. When Ruthie was little, she had adored her father. Her mother was harsh and cruel and complained all the time. Nothing was ever good enough for her mother, not even her husband. Ruthie remembered her father coming home exhausted from a hard day at work. Her mother would nag and nag until he did the chores she wanted done and then took her out for dinner. Even when they returned, her mother was miserable.

She never remembered her mother smiling. Mother hated their small house and wanted a bigger one. She wanted new clothes that Ruthie's father couldn't afford. Nothing her father did could make her mother happy.

Little as she was, Ruthie could feel her father's sadness. He would sit in his chair and stare out the window. His eyes would have a faraway look as if he were dreaming of a happier place. The little girl would bring her father his paper or his cup of coffee. He was grateful and would seem happy for a few minutes, but the sadness would quickly return. And then there was that day, the worse day of Ruthie's life.

Her parents had been fighting all that Saturday morning. Her mother was screaming about how much she had given up to marry a loser. Usually her father just sat and listened sadly to her mother's ranting. This time was different. This time, he screamed back. His answers seemed to make her mother madder. She said worse and worse things. Eight-year-old Ruthie covered her ears and wept. She wanted her mother to stop. She knew something bad was going to happen.

When her father packed his suitcase and tossed it in his car, Ruthie begged him not to leave. He was so busy shouting that he paid no attention to the little girl. As he pulled out of the driveway, Ruthie ran after him. She ran as fast as she could, following him halfway up the block. The car was too fast. She couldn't catch up. Running, out of breath, she collapsed on the sidewalk as he disappeared. Ruthie never saw her father again.

She hated her mother, blaming her for chasing her father away. She vowed she would never be like her demanding mother and she kept her vow. Ruthie never demanded anything of the men in her life.

Ruthie got up from the booth as Tom continued to stare out the window. He hardly noticed when she left. *Maybe this time will be different*, Ruthie thought as she waited on another customer. *Maybe this time I will be the one to walk away first.* Ruthie thought of the long, lonely years stretching before her. *Will I ever find a man who'll love me enough to stay?*

Returning to where Billy and Angie now sat coloring a new picture, Ruthie sat beside her youngest boy.

"Angie, how did you know that Tom was just like all the others?"

It took Angie a few minutes to understand what Ruthie meant. Sometimes, it took her a moment to connect with the meaning behind the words.

"Look eyes. You talk, he look. Then right away look out. Look at road like Billy look at cookie. Old boyfriend, same eyes," answered Angie as the waitress looked at the blond man with fresh discernment.

Ruthie sighed, "You know, Angie, you're right. My last boyfriend had the same look in his eyes. Grabbing a rag to wipe the crumbs off the table, Ruthie sighed loudly. "Maybe I'll just skip this heartache before it happens."

Angie smiled. "That good. Need man feet on ground. Need man see just you."

Ruthie laughed sarcastically. "Yeah, but where a man is like that?"

Angie shouted as she jumped up to leave, "Oh he is round, just wait. Bye now, gotta go."

Billy waved as he watched his friend ride away.

Six

At my first defense no one appeared on my behalf, but everyone deserted me. May it not be held against them! But the Lord stood by me and gave me strength, so that through me the proclamation might be completed and all the Gentiles might hear it. And I was rescued from the lion's mouth. (2 Tim. 4:16-17)

People commonly believe that hate is the opposite of love. That is simply not true. Hate involves anger, resentment, and strong emotion. It denotes a strong disturbing sense of the other. There is a spiritual tie in the sensation of hatred. The hater has to care about the hated and how the hated feels. The two converge back and forth in a strange dance of passion. No, the opposite of love is apathy.

Lonely children are unaware of the many things they have never been taught or the love they have missed. Neglect is like a cold wind that chills the heart of the unwanted soul. The ignored child simply knows something is absent, but cannot articulate what is missing. Unfortunately such children usually think what is misplaced is within them.

When Tommy finished killing the baby birds, he walked to the front of the house only to see his family pulling out of the driveway.

His body lurched forward as his arms reached out. But he didn't move from the spot. It was as if the soles of his shoes were glued to the ground. It was his heart, which longed for love, which made him reach. Experience, including mockery and laughter, made him freeze. He almost called out, but the cry died in his throat.

Tommy watched the sedan's taillights as it disappeared up the road. Although he knew the door was probably locked, he checked. He still hoped that maybe, just maybe, they had thought about him. The tight doorknob proved otherwise.

He wandered aimlessly, carrying a long stick that he poked at the picket fences along the picturesque street. The homes glowed with warmth and plenty. His own home fit right in the quaint style. Tommy wondered what secrets each house hid behind their ornate front doors.

"Get that stick off my fence," the white-haired woman yelled as he passed her house. He had learned that most adults were stunned by dirty language and she was shocked by the curse words he used. It gave him the chance to get away. Running down the sidewalk, he looked back to see her shocked expression. He kept running, not giving her a chance to recognize him. Joe's beatings were harsh on any given day. However, when another adult complained about Tommy, the beatings were unbearable. Joe didn't want to draw any attention.

Tommy was out of breath as he slowed. His body was coated with a slick sweat. He was heated as he caught his breath. Still, without a jacket, he felt a chill run through his thin body, despite the unusual warmth of the February day.

He wandered toward Main Street thinking the stores would be open and warm on such a Saturday. He eased into the hardware store. He loved the last aisle at the back of the store. Fresh-water fishing poles of various colors and sizes lined the wall, beckoning to him. He found the feathered flies and spools of line fascinating. Tommy let his hand stroke the tapered poles. The sensation of the smooth fiberglass comforted him.

During trout season, Tommy had seen boys fishing with their fathers down at the lake. The poles whistled through the air with grace. Fathers guided the hands of the youngest until they developed their skills. How he longed to have a father to teach him. Some of the older boys that Tommy hung with were unavailable during fishing season. They were spending their free time fishing with their fathers and friends.

Tommy dreamed of buying his own pole one day. As he guided his hand along the smooth shaft of one of the more expensive poles, Tommy closed his eyes. Holding the pole, he imagined a tug on the line. He could smell the pines that surrounded the lake and hear the lapping of the water as the trout took the bait. His was about to make a sharp tug on the pole when the voice shattered his dream.

"Hey kid, keep your paws off the merchandise!" the owner gruffly shouted.

Tommy, pulled from his daydream, turned with anger, and stared at the owner of the hardware store.

"Someday, I'm going to get you," answered Tommy with as little emotion in his voice as he could muster.

Leaving the store, Tommy resolved that he would kill that man one day. He strolled around the Main Street feeling unwelcome wherever he went. He watched a family walking hand-in-hand, sharing a fun Saturday morning. He watched the father with his arm draped over his son's shoulder. It denoted a sense of pride in the ownership of his boy. *Why can't someone love me?* wondered the disheveled boy. *There must be something wrong with me.*

"I'm just like my old man," Tommy whispered to himself as he looked longingly at the buns and pies in the bakery window. His stomach growled with hunger as he pulled open the glass door.

The bakery was crowded, filled with people holding numbered tickets, awaiting their Saturday morning treats. Tommy pulled a number from the ticket machine, but he had no intention of waiting. While one of the salesgirls took a special order for a birthday cake , and the other turned her back to fill a bag with crumb buns, Tommy slowly worked his way through the crowd. He found his way next to the spinning refrigerated case that displayed cream-filled treats.

Tommy eyed the crowd. One man was studying the contents of the case, so he waited. When the man turned around, Tommy scanned the store again. Everyone seemed lost in thought, planning what to order when their number was called. Tommy quickly opened the case and grabbed two chocolate-covered éclairs. He shoved them in his pocket and looked around to see if anyone had noticed. No one had.

He didn't run out immediately. That would look suspicious, he thought as he slowly made his way toward the front. He scanned the glass case filled with butter-cream cakes as if he were deciding what he wanted. Edging along the counter, he finally reached the door and made a quick escape.

Striding down the sidewalk, Tommy took his time. He wanted to blend in with the Saturday browsers. *Never call attention to yourself,* he thought as he reached the edge of the small town. Sitting on the curb in front of a large Victorian, the boy had no fear of being disturbed. The crazy woman who lived here was a shut-in, insane since the death of her son many years ago. Tommy had only seen her once on mischief night, when he and a few of the older boys had egged the house. The peculiar woman had come out on the porch to yell at them. Knowing she would never go past the porch, the boys had taunted her, calling her names like Ghost Woman and Graveyard Grannie. It had been a hoot.

Sitting on the curb in front of the house, Tommy crammed the stolen sweets into his mouth. Devouring them quickly, he licked his lips and sticky fingers in delight. This took the edge off his hunger and Tommy was always hungry. He was about to leave, when he heard a pup crying.

The puppy yelped in short spurts, punctuated by whining. Tommy pushed through the bushes that bordered the front fence of the house. The thick bush scratched his face and thorns and bristles stabbed his ankles, but Tommy didn't care. He was used to pain.

Pushing the brush aside, he kept his cover well. He had just enough room to peer through the picket fence hidden by the overgrown shrub.

Peeking around, he spotted the puppy on the side porch, in front of the back door. It seemed lost, whining for help.

The mother must have abandoned it. What a stupid mutt, thought the boy as he imagined taking the puppy down to the lake and holding it under the water. It must be the runt of the litter, he mused as he laughed at the whining pup. Tommy had heard about animals. They sometimes refused to feed the runt. They saved their milk for the healthy babies. In nature, the runts were ignored, left to die.

"Someone should put the thing out of its misery," he whispered under his breath. Tommy was about to sneak down to the side porch and grab the pup, when he heard the side door creak open. He watched as the odd lady of the house bent down and picked up the puppy. He laughed to himself as she looked around and then cooed over the canine. When she took the pup into the house, Tommy realized he had lost the opportunity to have fun with the puppy. Pulling away, he headed down the walk. Perhaps he could find someone at the park.

Tommy walked down to the lake at the center of the park, on the edge of town. The older boys, the ones Tommy hung with, liked to ice skate on the winter lake. After hiking the few blocks down to the park, he was disappointed to find the lake's icy cover had been weakened by the unseasonably warm winter. A large, white sign warned that the ice was too thin for skating and even walking on the lake was forbidden.

Tommy sighed at yet another disappointment. Finding a hidden grove among a circle of scrub pines, he shivered despite the warm air. Renewed hunger stabbed at his ribs as he sat alone. There was no place for him. No place for him to go. He sighed again as he contemplated another empty weekend.

That's when he noticed the squirrel as it stopped along the edge of the frozen lake. Picking up a rock, he inched his way toward the rodent as it stood on its hind legs. Inch by inch, Tommy stopped and started on his stomach. In military style, he crawled along as silently as he could. A film of perspiration coated his forehead as he approached his unwary victim.

Creeping closer, Tommy skimmed the rock at the squirrel with great precision. As the boy planned, the rock hit the squirrel. He wanted the squirrel to run out on the ice hoping it might drown and he could watch. Taken by surprise, it did run onto the ice. Light as a feather, it ran quickly along the perimeter and up the nearest tree.

Frustrated, Tommy studied the lake. In some areas the ice seemed thick and supportive. However, in the full sun, the surface not protected by the pines was cracked and thin. Tommy returned to the grove, sitting where he had a full view of the lake. The squirrel's escape had annoyed him. He would just wait until a better victim came along.

Seven

He said to them, "The harvest is abundant but the laborers are few; so ask the master of the harvest to send out laborers for his harvest. Go on your way; behold, I am sending you like lambs among wolves. Carry no money bag, no sack, no sandals, and greet no one along the way. (Luke 10:2-5)

A prisoner looking through the bars of his cell knows he is trapped, limited by the dimensions of his chamber. In this knowledge, he is better off than most of humanity. Unaware, so many are in captivity. Imprisoned by fear that paralyzes, or anger that blinds, so many forget the dreams of childhood. Some people are ruled by greed or tormented by envy – traits that shrivel a spirit into such smallness, until it is lost.

Ensnared in a misshaped body and slow mind, Angie was less captive than most. At moments, her spirit glowed so brightly, the joy overflowed. She shrieked as the bike kept rolling. The wind chilled her face as she clung to the handlebars. It was a sharp decline, just at the end of Main Street. When she turned the corner, the sidewalk tilted into a hill. As the bike left the rise, it built up speed. She kicked her legs out, away from the pedals, and the bike ran on momentum alone. It was a thrill for her to experience such velocity.

As the sidewalk leveled, the bike slowed and placed her at the gate of her next customer, Mrs. Schmidt. Except in poorer weather, this lady continuously sat on her front porch. Angie climbed off her bike. She never threw a paper if she could hand it to someone.

"Hi, Mrs. Schmidt. You have good day?" Angie asked as she gave the tabloid to the woman.

"Oh my, yes. It's so warm for February. Just a heavy sweater and I can sit out on the porch. I remember winters when I was a girl in this house. The snow was so high, we couldn't even open the front door."

"Wow!" exclaimed Angie as she tried to imagine such a thing. "Did you no school when it snowed?" Angie smiled, remembering the few snow days she had enjoyed."

Mrs. Schmidt had a mellow laugh, soft and melodious. Angie grinned even though she didn't know what was so funny.

"Oh, no! We had school even when it snowed. You see, my mother was the teacher," she said, her face glowing.

"Too bad for you," Angie shot back.

The woman smiled, pushing a strand of white hair from her forehead, "That's what my brother, Daniel, used to say. He said it wasn't fair. Whenever we had to work, he would announce that he wished to be adopted by a family that didn't set such store in books."

"You brother?" asked the young girl.

The older woman answered wistfully, "I used to have a brother, Daniel. He died in the war years ago. Now I haven't any family, except my cats."

"No worry, you very old. See Daniel soon," Angie announced.

Mrs. Schmidt's eyes opened wide. Color rose in her face as she stared at Angie. Then her face softened and the corners of her mouth rose in a smile, "Why I guess you're right. I hope I will be seeing Daniel shortly. I hope I see all the people I used to know. It's hard to outlive your family and friends. I worry about my cats. Will I see them after I die?

"No worry. God made cat. Loves them. Take long time. Moma

says cat live nine times. Gotta go now. Lots of paper today." Angie walked to her bike while waving. "See next week."

Angie pedaled to the neighbor's house. Slowing as she reached the lawn, she took a paper and threw it. Each week she would aim for the porch and each week she would miss.

A gruff-looking man opened the door and yelled, "Stupid girl, can't you ever get the paper on the steps?"

She didn't answer, but stuck her tongue out at the man. Moma called him an old crab. He stuck his tongue out at Angie. Grumbling, he picked up his paper and went in his house, slamming the door. It was the same every week. Angie pedaled to her next customer.

The church sat among the gravestones of its deceased members, its steeple rising above the buildings of the town. A newly built rectory stood in stark contrast, attached to the historic building. Angie didn't throw the papers for this customer. Reverend Stephen Huber took ten papers, which he placed in the vestibule of the church for his parishioners.

Carefully counting twice, she tallied ten papers and placed them in her canvas bag. She kicked the bicycle stand into place even though the training wheels held the bike upright. Josh had taught her in preparation for the day she could balance the bike herself.

Angie rang the bell and entered the unlocked rectory office. No one was there. It was the first time this had happened and she didn't know what to do. She looked longingly at the bowl on the desk, which held the lollipops. Angie really wanted a red one, but was afraid to touch them without Reverend Huber's permission. That be stealing, she thought as she walked down the hall that connected the rectory to the church. *Moma always says not to touch anything not yours,* thought the girl.

Happy to find the pastor in the church, she tiptoed. She didn't want to interrupt the minister's prayer. She smiled at the angels surrounding the youthful minister. The only other person Angie knew with three angels was Father Hughes. She moved tentatively, but still the minister heard her and looked up. She was upset to see tears.

"Why you crying?" Angie blurted out. "Did you get a hurt?"

The minister smiled. "Oh, no, Angie, I just was talking to God about a problem. I don't mean to worry you."

"I no worry. Moma say it sin to worry. Jesus take care all."

Reverend Huber rubbed the long scar on his cheek and laughed. "I wish my congregation knew as much about Jesus as Moma. It would make my job simple."

"Oh, Moma know it all. She knows all the poems." Angie clapped her hand to her mouth quickly. She had never told anyone about the poems.

The minister regarded her quizzically. "What do you mean, Angie? What poems?"

The girl knew that she put the cat in the bag as Moma liked to say. She couldn't find any easy way not to tell the minister. Haltingly, she told the story of the poems. Reverend Huber sat in the pew as she explained what Moma taught her to keep other children from hurting her.

Angie explained with relish, "Like when Tommy says 'you stupid', Moma tell me poem."

"What's the rest of the poem?" the minister asked.

Angie stood up tall and inhaled deeply to add volume to her recitation. "Stupid, stupid so you say, I was made in God's best way!"

The minister seemed fascinated with Angie's narrative, "Tell me some more of the poems your Moma taught you."

She knew the poems so well now. Tommy never kicked her again as he had done on the first day of school. Tommy Ellis still called out those words, but the other children had given up since Angie knew the answers. Moma had taught her well.

Reverend Huber was smiling broadly as Angie finished her story.

"You done crying?" she asked.

"Yes, Angie. I guess my problems are small. You showed me how tiny they are."

"What you problem?" the girl asked, tilting her head to the side.

"I am trying to write a sermon, one to reach the hearts of my congregation."

"You done?" Angie asked.

The cheerless man answered, "I'm done. I don't know how good it is, but I finished it an hour ago."

"I hear?" she dramatically pointed to her ears as she sat in the front pew.

Reverend Huber started to protest, but answered, "Why not? It will give me a chance to practice. Besides Angie, you may be the only one interested in the talk. Okay, I'll get the papers off my desk." He smiled as he headed toward his office. "I'll get you a lollipop, also. Do you mind taking a red one? I have too many of the cherry ones."

Excited, she clapped her hands. "Oh, sure. Red one good by me!"

She looked around the church as she waited. The walls and pews were a clean white. The red carpet contrasted well with the fresh look of the church. The stained-glass windows scattered the sunlight into rainbow prisms, splayed across the rug. Angie liked this church and the kind minister with the three angels.

Reverend Huber returned with the sermon. "Here, Angie, could you do me a favor and take two red lollipops? I have too many."

She hopped up and down in her seat and took the lollipops. Pushing one in her blue-jean pocket, she answered, "I save one Josh, Okay? I eat mine now."

Angie rapidly removed the paper and stuck the cherry pop in her mouth as the minister made his way to the podium. He began his talk in a pleasing voice. Quietly, she sat and listened.

When he'd finished, the young minister smiled at the girl who made up his audience. "What do you think of it?"

"It good! Jesus loves. Moma says every day," Angie answered.

"Moma is a sharp woman. I would like to meet her one day." the minister replied.

"Oh Moma cat-o-lick like me. We go Father Hughes. I like you. You talk good," the young girl announced.

Reverend Huber chuckled. "For the first time in my life I'm envious of Father Hughes. He has astonishing parishioners."

Silently, she watched as he sat beside her. His smile faded and the lines in his forehead deepened. Angie thought the dark-haired man would be so handsome, like Josh, if he didn't have the deep scar running down his face. When he was upset, the scar turned a deeper purple. Lost in his worries, the minister seemed to forget she was still beside him. She hated seeing her friend in pain.

"Why you sad?" She bent her head, perplexed.

Defeated, his shoulders slumped. He sighed. "My sermon doesn't even matter. I want to tell others of the mercy of Jesus. They should know their sins can be forgiven and they can have peace and everlasting life, but no one comes. The congregation diminished when I came to replace Reverend Heffner. Those who were faithful to the previous minister preferred a gospel of sin and punishment. My sermons on the love and mercy of Jesus disappointed them. Now there are even fewer participants. Oh, a few of the older congregation still show up, but the church seems empty." Angie felt so sorry for him.

He continued, "When I first came here, I had hope. I wanted to reach out to the children. I wanted to reach the lonely child, the child who didn't have love at home. I wanted to create a safe haven for the abused and unwanted. It's hopeless."

Angie watched as a single tear ran down the man's cheek. She saw one of the three angels place an arm of comfort around the broken man. The angel reached up and wiped the tear away. Angie saw the angels smiling at her.

The minister said, "I'm sorry, Angie. I don't know why I'm telling you all this. There isn't anything you can do. I just find it easy to talk to you."

She smiled. "No worry. People no come you, you go them."

Angie watched as Reverend Huber sat upright. His eyes widened and he reached up and rubbed his ears unconsciously as if he hadn't heard right. The minister turned and stared at the girl beside him. Angie sat quietly beside the minister and said a prayer in her heart for the sad man. Afterwards, her attention lost focus. She rocked her feet back and forth, fascinated with the swing of her red sneakers. It was a few minutes before she looked back at the minister.

"What did you just say, Angie?" Reverend Huber's voice was husky with emotion.

At first, she seemed confused and then she remembered. "People no come you, you go them."

Remembering how late she was, she got up and waved to her friend as he remained, sitting silently. She headed out the church door and to her bike.

Reverend Stephen Huber wondered why the Lord had guided him to such a dying church filled with elderly parishioners. He wanted to work with children. He wanted to come to the aid of abused children. Whenever he thought about the pain of hurting children, the memories of his own childhood rose up. He tried to bury the pain, but it was impossible. The deep, purple scar that marred his face was a daily reminder.

His father had been walking rage, a large, muscle-bound man who usually ignored his family, but walked with the Spirit of Anger as a daily companion. He lashed out verbally and physically on a weekly basis. The house Stephen grew up in was quiet. Not because of peace, but because he and his mother walked on eggshells, trying to be unnoticed and unobtrusive. His strongest memory of his mother was of her holding her finger up to pursed lips, reminding him not to disturb his father.

When his father was disturbed, the quiet of the house shattered into an explosive heat. His father's anger was always directed toward his mother. Without warning, the red-faced man would reach across the table and slap her. That was on a good day. Often the abuse became close-fisted. She would just stand there, moving between Stephen and his father. That was until that night, the night that

Stephen turned sixteen.

His mother had baked a cake for a small celebration. Just for the family, as no one ever came to the house. After dinner she set the table for three and proudly brought Stephen's favorite, strawberry shortcake with lit candles, from the kitchen. His father just sat there. He seemed alright, but they should have known better. Stephen's mother cut the cake with great fanfare and, as was the tradition, gave the birthday boy the first slice. She never saw it coming.

His father slapped her across the face. Stunned she silently reached up to the blood that drizzled from her nose.

"Is he the man of the house?" His father spat out the words. "Is he the one who gives you a paycheck each week?" The man lifted up the cake and smashed it against the wall. "There's your happy birthday, son" he said sarcastically.

Stephen couldn't explain what happened next. It had been a night just like any other night in the Huber home. His mother stood there frozen. She never talked back, but something changed within her. Without a word, and almost mindlessly, she fingered the large knife, grasping the handle. With a growing look of discernment, his father moved. Grabbing her hand, he applied pressure until she dropped the dagger, then pushed her against the wall.

Stephen didn't remember how he ended up with the knife in his hand, but as he came toward his father, the man whirled around and grabbed him.

"You want to take on your old man, do you?" he demanded as he held Stephen's arm immobile. Slapping Stephen across the face, his father knocked him to the ground. Suddenly, Stephen's mother stepped forward as if to protect her son.

"Oh, you want to protect your baby. Well, here you go! You should be able to spot him in a crowd now," he crowed. Taking the knife, he slashed Stephen across the face. The large blade cut a quarter-inch gash down from the forehead to the jaw. If Stephen had not instinctively closed his eyes, he would have lost his right eye. Dropping the weapon, the old man stomped out the front door.

Headed toward the bar, he never looked back.

Stephen's mother rushed to her son with a towel and, later ice, but never had the courage to take him to the emergency room for stitches.

"Come, Mom, let's get out of here!" Stephen cried.

His mother tried to soothe him. "And just where would we go?"

"Well, let's at least call the police and get him in jail," begged the boy as his mother attempted to stop the bleeding.

"That would just make things worse. Calm down. He'll be sorry in the morning," she insisted.

Stephen didn't answer. Looking back, he wished with all his heart he had dragged her out. Later that night, after the wound had stopped bleeding and when his parents were asleep, he packed a small knapsack and left. He never returned.

Three years later, Stephen found himself nervously sitting in an ornate outer office. His whole life was riding on the next hour. He had worked long hours washing dishes and attending night school. He had succeeded with straight A's and dreamed of becoming a minister.

Looking down, Stephen watched his hands tremble. His stomach whirled with panic. He was waiting for an interview with the dean for a full-time scholarship to divinity school. He knew that if he didn't overcome his apprehension, the interview would not go well. Picking up the newspaper, he thought the distraction would calm him.

Flipping through his hometown newspaper, he found himself scanning the obituaries. His mother's name jumped out at him. The obit stated that she had died after lengthy illness.

She was ill and I never went to see her. Did she call for me? Did she die alone? The pain cut his heart as the knife had cut his face. Stephen had never gone home to help her. He had just saved himself. Never again would those soft, brown eyes look at him with love. Never again would he see the sweet, gentle smile that graced her face. *Too late*, his heart cried. *Too late to see her*, his soul screamed.

Suddenly, he was called and seated before the dean. What was asked and what he answered was a blur. All he knew was that he received the full scholarship within the week.

He never went back for the funeral. Stephen couldn't imagine what might happen if he saw his father. *What good would that do? Would it bring her back?* For years, nightmares of his mother calling for him from a sick bed penetrated his sleep. Stephen would awaken in the middle of the night, his bed sheets wet from his sweat. Lying there, he would think of all the many things he could have said or done to make her last years happier. He felt as if he was losing his mind.

It was in prayer that he finally made peace with the truth. He couldn't go back. He couldn't put adult thoughts in a 16-year-old mind. He couldn't have saved his mother, but he could save others.

Stephen worked hard and graduated a full minister. The young man resolved he would help other children. No child should ever watch his mother suffer. No child should ever feel alone with nowhere to turn, but his dream was frustrated in this parish. No one came. Everything he had worked for had become so hopeless. Then the Lord had sent a child.

Falling to his knees, he wept. Kneeling in front of the altar, the minister praised the Lord, as three angels rejoiced beside him. *Of course, why hadn't he seen it?* The Lord promised a child would lead them. Today that word proved true. *Why hadn't he thought of it?* It was all so simple.

Simple, yet brilliant enough to be the words of the Holy Spirit, the minister realized. *If they didn't come to him, he must go to them.*

Eight

Yet I live, no longer I, but Christ lives in me. (Gal. 2:20)

Those who suffer often feel alone. It seems that the world marches to its own beat, leaving those who are slow, ill, or just plain tired by the wayside. There is no time to stop. Destiny awaits and the future is for the ready. Slowing down to look around is not an option. We have all heard the famous expression – Time waits for no man. Unfortunately, that usually means that no man can wait for another. No man can stop long enough to notice another's suffering.

There had been a dark and dismal day that changed the destiny of every man. Yet, many hurried by. They had chores to attend and marketing to do before sundown. So many people hurried past Calvary.

Elderly Father Hogan stared at his lunch with little appetite. The tall priest swirled his fork mindlessly through the rice and beans. He had eaten the same meal twice a day for the last week and had no desire to eat it again. Memories of his mother's kitchen filled his mind, teasing his appetite.

His mother, Maggie, was from the village of Ahascragh in County Galway. A sprite of a woman, she loved to cook. Father Hogan's mouth watered with reminiscences of delicate boxty that melted in his mouth. In his mind, he could smell the bubbling Coddle in her cast-iron pan. She loved to tell of the shock she had when she first came to the U. S. She had never heard of corned beef and cabbage. Maggie Hogan would give a delicate laugh as she shook her head.

"In the old country, the people used to put the ham on the bottom of the pot. My grandmother covered it with cabbage and potatoes. When I asked her why, she said it was what the Irish did to hide the meat from the English. The meat was put deep down in the boiling water and the cabbage killed the smell of the sweet ham," Maggie explained and laughed. "If the English knew the family had meat, they would raise the rent or lower the wages. Ah . . . but corned beef, that's all American," Maggie Hogan announced in a thick brogue.

She had come from a part of Ireland that still spoke the native language. She often mixed the Irish and English together, especially while yelling at her rambunctious family of six children. Father Hogan was the youngest of the tribe and the only one left alive. He had sadly buried each one of his brothers and sisters. He still had many nieces and nephews, but they were scattered all over the country and he seldom saw them. It seemed he was only called on for ceremonial occasions, such as weddings or baptisms, but he didn't resent it. They were young and had busy lives of their own. He was just the old uncle after all.

Thinking of his mother always brought a smile to his face. Even as a child he appreciated her stamina and strength. It was a treat to watch her. She ran her home like a conductor of an orchestra, with passion and joy. But he remembered her greatest joy was on the day she took her vow to become an American citizen. Dressed in her best suit, she raised her hand with such pride, her son had never forgotten it.

Looking down to the bland and now lukewarm plate of beans, the memories faded. However, his body, overly thin, needed the protein and carbohydrates. He pushed a forkful in his mouth and chewed. Forgetting the monotony of the meal, the priest stared out the rectory window that overlooked the winter-bare gardens spanning to the road.

Laughing, he spotted Angie as she pedaled up to the rectory. *She's late. I wonder what stories she has today*, pondered the elderly priest as he walked over to open the door. Angie struggled to hold the pile of 15 papers that Father wanted for the vestibule. Father Hogan was quick to relieve her of her burden.

"Come in, Angie," invited the priest as he placed the papers on the side table. "Would you like a glass of pop?"

"Yeah, me tired!" answered Angie. Taking a deep breath, she sat at the long, pine table as Father Hogan poured her a glass of soda.

"So, Angie, what's the latest?" asked Father Hogan as he sat across the table. "You always have great stories about the townsfolk." Angie gulped down half of the glass with loud slurps. "Whoa, now, Angie, take your time or you'll choke," the priest cautioned.

"I so thirst-eee," declared Angie, as she wiped her mouth with the back of her hand. Father Hogan laughed with delight. Most people put on such airs when they were around the priest, but Angie was so natural.

Father Hogan loved to talk to Angie. He had no way of knowing how happy Angie's visits made the three angels that she saw around him. She shared the story of the minister, ending with a new thought.

"Maybe, we go old church Sunday. Be protest," she announced.

Father Hogan smiled. "You mean Protestant. I wish we could. It's a kind thought, Angie."

"You doing nothing Saturday?" she asked

"Next Saturday, why?" asked the priest.

"You maybe marry!" smiled Angie.

"Angie, you know that priests can't marry."

Angie's face crinkled up in puzzlement. Then her mouth dropped with understanding,

"Oh, you no marry. You marry Harold and Ruthie. I tell Harold what to do."

"Tell me, what did you do?" asked the delighted priest. Angie quickly related her story about the truck driver's moving feet. Father Hogan laughed so hard that he started to cry.

Angie looked carefully at the priest. "You no eat. Food get cold"

The priest looked at his plate and sighed.

"I'm just sick of rice and beans," he announced.

"No eat that," suggested Angie. "Eat hot dog." She smiled, proud of another solution.

"It's not that easy. You see, I'm saving money for something special."

Angie looked puzzled, then grinned with a new understanding. "Oh, me know, you have face sewed up too. Your face cracked."

The priest looked confused. "What do you mean?"

Angie took another sip of pop, swallowed quickly, and answered, "Mrs. Pulaski got old car. It smoke and pop. She kick it when me come. Me say go get good car. She say no. Got save money." Angie smiled at her long story.

Sensing there was more to the story, the old priest asked, "Why is she saving money?"

"Oh," replied Angie, "She need new face. Old face all cracked!"

Taking both hands, Angie pulled at the sides of her own face until her features were stretched and grotesque. "She say doctor sew it up. So no cracks."

Father Hogan laughed long and hard. "What do you think of that?" he asked.

Angie stared back at the priest. "You got cracks. Maybe doc can sew up. Me tell her let hair grow. Get tight ponytail."

Father Hogan was delighted. Angie's visit was one of the highlights of his lonely life. He used to be in a large parish, with several other priests. They had shared both the joy and sorrow of serving a large community. However, since he had been made pastor of this much smaller congregation, he suffered the loneliness of isolation. Angie filled some of his time with joy.

"Why do you think Mrs. Pulaski wants to spend all her money, and go through all that pain, just to get rid of the cracks in her face?" asked the priest.

Angie looked puzzled, then her face lit up. "Me think she be lonely. She live all by self in big house. Maybe find husband with no cracks."

Father Hogan chuckled. "You may be right. People do strange things when they're lonely. Are you ever lonely?"

Angie's face grew sad. "Me got Moma and Josh. Me lonely for Mommy. No Mommy for Angie."

The priest stopped laughing and looked carefully at the forlorn child before him. "It's good to have a mother to talk to. I miss my own mother. She's in heaven like yours."

Angie looked up. "What you do when miss her?"

Father Hogan got up and went to the sideboard. Opening the drawer, he removed a holy card and placed it before the girl. "When I'm lonely for my mother, I talk to Mary, the mother that Jesus gave us. Here take this card. You can look at it and talk to Mary anytime."

Angie picked up the holy card with care and saw it depicted Mary holding a lamb and the child Jesus. "Oh she be so beautiful. She have time for Angie?"

Father smilingly assured the child, "Jesus gave her to us. She has always had time to listen to me. I think she's happy to listen to those who don't have a mother on earth."

Angie stared at the lace-edged card with love. "Me take good care. Thanks."

She carefully placed the card in her back pocket and turned to the priest.

Looking at the now cold rice and beans that the priest swirled with his fork, she asked unexpectedly, "Why you save?"

"Oh, it's a secret," he answered quickly

Angie's face fell in disappointment. He couldn't bear to see his little friend so crushed.

"Do you know what a secret is?" he asked,

Jumping up and down in her seat, Angie announced, "Oh yeah.

Me good keep secret. Never tell." She clamped her hands over her mouth as if to emphasize her silence.

"Okay, if you promise never to tell, I'll explain. I'm giving up desserts, and meat, and lots of good things to save money for a poor family that doesn't have enough food," the priest told the interested girl.

"You learn from Bible, Jesus!" answered Angie in wonder.

Father Hogan laughed. "Well I should have. But I actually learned the secret from a movie." Angie looked confused.

"It was an old movie that I saw many years ago. It was called *Magnificent Obsession*," explained the priest.

"It God movie?" asked Angie.

"I guess in a way it was. Although it never mentions God, it tells how to live a life as Jesus taught. It's the story of a very selfish man who only cared about having fun. In the story, he's responsible for the death of a man he hardly knows. As he learns about how good the man was, he wants to learn to live just like the good man," explained the priest.

"How he live?" asked Angie, mesmerized.

"Oh, at first, he does it all wrong. He does try to do good for people, but he wants everyone to know. He wants them to be grateful, to like him for his good works."

"That not way?" asked Angie.

"No. The whole idea is to do the good in secret. In the Bible, Jesus says that when we give, we should not let the left hand know what the right hand is doing," he explained.

Looking over, he could see he had confused the child, "The secret of this happiness is to do all the good in secret. Everyday try to do good for someone without letting them know who did it. Then they have only God to thank. It's all about the secret. It is so much fun to watch what people need and secretly help them. It makes you happy. That way, you can hardly wait to do some good each day. That's why it's called a magnificent obsession."

He was surprised to see Angie's face had reddened with anger.

She banged on the table.

"Me no good. Everyone know cakes from Angie. Me want do mag . . . mag . . ."

Father Hogan suggested, "You can just call it a "happy habit." Maybe you could help me. I want to give this money to the family that needs food, but I don't want them to know I gave it."

Angie grew excited. "Me help. Me give. No let see!"

"That would be great, Angie. Do you know the Martinez family that lives in the yellow house on the corner by the railroad track?"

"Yes, Angie know. In school them."

"Do you think you could give them this envelope, without them seeing?" the priest asked, as he took a hundred-dollar bill, wrapped it in paper, and sealed it in an envelope.

"Yes, me can!" announced Angie.

Growing solemn, Angie's eyes opened wide as she regarded the priest. "You be saint."

Father Hogan looked at Angie and chuckled. "No, I wish I were. You see, Angie, most of the time giving in secret makes me very happy. But sometimes I am just like that selfish man in the movie. I want people to know. I want them to be grateful. Sometimes I'm sorry about giving up so much. I try to save from my pay, but a priest doesn't make a lot of money. I get sad that nobody knows how much I suffer. No one knows how it feels."

Angie took the envelope and, tucking it in her pocket, she answered, "You wrong. He know." She pointed to the large crucifix on the wall of the kitchen. "He see." Angie smiled and waved as she rushed out the door, excited about her mission to deliver the money.

Father Hogan sat stunned for more than 15 minutes. Looking up to the crucified Jesus, he wept. *Of course, He knows. He knows all about suffering. He sees it all.*

Nine

Be self-controlled and alert. Your enemy the devil prowls around like a roaring lion looking for someone to devour. (1 Peter 5:8, NIV)

We are spiritual beings incarnate. Our souls live this life encased in a body that has all the ancient instincts of our wild, earthly companions. A tingle rides up our spine or a chill washes over us when a threat is lurking around the corner. However, we have become so civilized, we often ignore the instincts that kept our ancestors alive for centuries. We allow reason to override the sense of danger that often forewarns us of a time of peril. The feeling that something is just not right should never be disregarded. Instinct is a gift from God.

Angie rode her bike across town, to the south of St. Veronica's church. The neighborhood started to change here. Instead of the superbly restored homes north of the church, these houses grew smaller and closer together. These blocks were lined with ranches and Cape Cods built in the fifties. Most of the yards were contained by old, chain link fences that held the numerous canine residents in check. Although small, these homes were still neat and clean, unlike the homes on the other side of the park. Most of the townsfolk looked at these few blocks as an introduction to the poorer side of town.

She hid her bike in the tall weeds of an abandoned lot. *It be no good they hear me*, she thought as she walked along the train tracks. The tracks were old and rusted. The weeds that grew between the ties testified to the long abandonment by the railroad. Walking along the track took her to the back of the Martinez home. The bright, yellow ranch displayed a large, vegetable garden in the backyard.

Angie crouched in the tall grass behind the back fence. Juan and Roberto were playing catch as their toddler sister played with a broken baby doll.

"What me do?" Angie whispered to herself. She struggled with thoughts of how to get past the children without anyone seeing her. She wanted to put Father Hogan's envelope in the mailbox with the free paper. Angie watched from the tall weeds, and was about to give up, when she heard Mrs. Martinez call from the back door.

"Come on in. It's time for lunch."

The three children ran in, leaving Angie a clear path to the mailbox. Skirting past the side yard, she made it to the front mailbox, and shoved the paper and the envelope in alongside the mail. Taking a deep breath, she scurried back through the vacant lot, and reached her hidden bike in record time.

Angie rested for a moment, then smiled to herself. *Me be so smart*, thought the self-satisfied child. Picking up her bike, she started off on the rest of her route in a joyful mood. Pausing for just a second, she almost made the turn toward the railroad tracks. Angie loved to ride right down the center of the ties. As she did she would let out a steady scream and the evenly placed bumps of the railroad ties would break up her scream until it became a chant. It was a small joy.

Angie was worried about how far the sun had advanced in the sky. It was almost afternoon. She thought she heard a soft voice whisper in her ear, a sort of angelic sigh. It was a gentle musing; the kind that often disguises itself as a thought.

The voice within seemed to say, "Take the long way. Go along the rails."

However, she was so late that she decided to take a shortcut. The girl turned to cut through the park.

Angie loved the park. Often in the winter, she would stop to watch the skaters on the lake. She tried, with Josh's help, to learn to skate each winter. Her sense of balance always landed her right on her backside. Josh would laugh, each time, as he helped her up. Her brother was a wonderful skater. He would allow her to hold onto his arm as he slowed to let her struggle around the lake. With his support, she felt just like one of the other kids.

Angie pedaled slowly along the gravel path that led to the lake. Today was such a warm and sunny day and sunlight glowed from a cloudless, blue sky. Looking up, she could see the light as it flickered between the barren branches of oak trees. She usually saw older people on benches and younger people jogging with their dogs. Yet, in spite of the beauty of the day, no one seemed to be enjoying the park at the moment. Today everyone seemed to be missing the smell of the pines and the sense of being one with nature.

Angie enjoyed waving to the people when she went to the park. It was a little eerie to ride for so long without seeing anyone. A sense of foreboding washed over her as the lake came into view. It was the same feeling she had when she woke up this morning.

Maybe me should have gone tracks, thought the girl as she slowed her bike. Looking at the lake, she felt an even a stranger sensation fluttering in her stomach. There was no one skating on the lake. It was so quiet. *Too quiet,* thought Angie. She stopped about a hundred yards from the lake and still didn't see anyone. She didn't see Tommy as he watched from the grove.

The girl had to go around the lake to reach the road that would lead her to her next stop, the community center. She stopped instinctually, but logically knew she had to continue. Concluding, she was just being silly, she told herself not to be a scare-dee cat out loud. Just the same, she decided to ride her bike faster to get out of the park. It just didn't feel right.

Angie had no way of knowing Tommy was watching her slow approach with relish. She didn't see when he started collecting the sharp rocks that lay on the ground like ammunition. Angie rode by, free of the knowledge that Tommy was loading up his pockets with the projectiles. A strange warning in her heart prompted her to increase her speed, which is why Tommy turned to see the determined girl pedal quickly by. She was already 200 yards ahead.

Tommy's primal scream pierced the silence of the park, startling her so that she looked back. Angie didn't see the rut in the road and her bike's front wheel struck it. She felt the bike falling, but it was too late. Crashing to the ground, the pain jolted her from the fear. Angie scraped along the gravel as blood gushed forth from both knees and her left elbow. Her bike tangled, with the front wheel turned the wrong way and the pedals spinning.

Looking up, she saw Tommy running toward her. Fright propelled her past the pain. Jumping up, the youngster ignored her bloody elbow and yanked at her bike. The training wheels had held in place, so she was able to set the bike upright. However, the front wheel had jammed, refusing to return to a forward position. Angie looked again and saw Tommy getting closer. She could feel her heart beating as if it would break right through the front of her chest. She gasped for air.

The angry boy was only 100 yards away and moving fast. Angie pulled hard on the handlebars and, finally, freed the wheel. She jumped onto her bike and, by the time she was pedaling, Tommy was within 50 yards of her. Angie pushed the pedals so hard that she was standing up as the bike reached full speed. Her knees ached, but she couldn't think about the pain. Harder and harder, she pushed with all her strength.

The bike took on a life of its own, flying down the gravel road that led to the park exit. In just a few minutes, she would reach the paved road leading to the community center. Somehow she knew once she reached the pavement, her bike would pick up so much speed that Tommy wouldn't be able to get her. She had managed to increase the distance between them and that infuriated Tommy. Looking back, Angie could see the anger in the boy's contorted face.

Panicked, she turned and realized she was just a few feet from paved roadway. A sense of safety washed over her, just before the rock hit the back of her head. The pain jolted her, pushing her head forward with the pressure of the strike. Angie's vision blurred with pain and the road before her became unnatural and wavy. She felt warm blood running down her neck and under the collar of her jacket. Dizzy, black spots appearing before her eyes, she continued on. The bike wobbled in a crooked line. She feared she might faint. Only panic kept her peddling.

For a moment, it seemed her slower pace gave Tommy the advantage. He closed the distance between them. He was reaching out to grab Angie, when she regained her composure. It seemed as if she was watching herself from a distance and, in fear, she reapplied pressure to get out of the park. With herculean effort, she pushed the bike to greater speed and precision.

The pursuing boy let out another scream of frustration as she increased the distance between them and made it to the roadway leading out of the park. Glancing behind her, Angie could see the boy as he slowed to a stop. His eyes were full of hatred as he watched Angie make her escape. She couldn't see the demons that belittled Tommy for letting her get away.

"Stupid idiot," whispered the smallest demon, "Stupid and slow, just like your old man."

The darkest demon spit in disgust as it whirled around the defeated child. "You let a dummy beat you. You're worthless!"

The boy let the rock he was holding slip from his hand as he turned back to the grove of pines where he had been hiding. The anger he felt toward Angie was now leveled at himself. He had failed to kill the worthless girl who made him feel so stupid with her poems. He had allowed a down to outsmart him. There was no hope for him. He was just like his old man. Tommy sat in frustration.

But the whispers continued and his mood brightened as the

swirl of darkness continued around him. Of course, it was not over. Of course, she would have to return this way. Tommy smiled. The next time he would be prepared.

Sister Val, as the children called her, heard the cries coming from the back of the center. Rushing to the industrial kitchen's screen door, the diminutive, Asian woman saw Angie as she dropped her bike and limped toward the entrance. Hurrying out to meet her, Sister Val placed her arm around the weeping child and led her into the kitchen.

"Me hate 'im," the child sobbed, as the woman sat her in a chair by the sink. Grabbing a clean, white cloth, she applied pressure to the back of the girl's head. Angie wept loudly.

"Hold this," Val instructed as she wet another cloth and cleaned the wounds on Angie's knees and elbow.

Grabbing the first aid kit from the far cabinet, Sister Val waited for her to calm down.

"Me hate 'im. He bad," cried the battered child.

"Who is he?" asked the woman.

"It be Tommy. Tommy scare me! Tommy hit me rock," the girl shrieked with rage.

"You mean a boy attacked you and threw rocks at you?" asked Sister Val.

"Tommy Ellis so mean! Me hate 'im," howled the girl as anger overwhelmed her.

Sister Val cleansed the numerous abrasions and applied antibiotic cream. Angie shook with emotion as Val wrapped bandages on her knees and elbow. Val was most concerned about the cut on the back of Angie's head. Head wounds, Val knew from experience, bled heavily. She was glad to see that the cut had stopped bleeding and wasn't very deep after all.

Angie shook with passion. "Tommy bad. So bad. Me wish him dead!"

"Hush, Angie," Sister Val whispered, hoping to calm the child, "You don't mean that. You can't wish anyone dead."

"Me mean!" she insisted as she pulled away in rage. "Me hate Tommy."

Ten

But because he wished to justify himself, he said to Jesus, "And who is my neighbor?" (Luke 10:29)

We are proud of our native land, taught to be grateful for the country that is our home. We wave flags at local parades and answer the call to service when our government calls. We learn the history of our country during our tender years. We watch the Olympics and root for our country's athletes. We just know in our hearts that our country is the best, the one that God favors. I wonder how all this looks to God. When He looks down on the earth He created, does He know where we have placed the borders?

Maria Martinez fed her children the buttered tortillas made from the last of the flour. She smiled bravely, hiding the fear of an empty purse and bare pantry. She ran out of money two weeks ago. The landlord had made a personal visit and doubled the rent of the small, yellow ranch. Unable to imagine uprooting the children again, she had paid the rent. Now with no money for food and wages a week away, she wondered if she had made the right decision.

"*Coma todo su alimento,*" ("Eat all your food,") she encouraged as the two boys continued to make jokes. They listened, not understanding her need to fill their stomachs. When they were done, she sent them outside with their younger sister and an admonition to keep a careful watch over her. After they bounded out the kitchen door to continue their play, Maria scraped the leftover waste from the plates with her fingers and swallowed the residue. The remnants hit her empty stomach without giving relief from the hunger pains. Instead, the paltry bits and pieces seemed to stimulate her body's longing for nourishment. As she washed the dishes, tears formed.

How had it come to this? she wondered.

A blanket of despondency settled over Maria and she couldn't shake the sorrow that overwhelmed her. Maria was a Poblanoes, a Mexican from the town of Pueblo, located between Mexico City and the port city of Vera Cruz. She ached for her family and her familiar home. Her elderly mother was still alive and lived in the home she used to share with her husband. *Would she ever see her mother or her home again?*

When Maria had to leave her mother behind, she was plagued with guilt. As the eldest girl, it was her responsibility to take care of her aging mother. Before she left, she had been assured by her four younger siblings that their mother would be watched over and financially maintained. She felt lost in this strange, cold land of a strange and, often cold, people.

Maria thought of her home in Pueblo, warm and familiar with a wonderful history. The tale of the founding of the city of Pueblo was an ancient legend of a long-dead bishop. The story was of his dream that told him where to build the city. While he slept one night, he dreamt of a valley with woods and a land full of fragrant meadows. The valley the bishop envisioned was cut by a river. In the dream, a group of heavenly angels descended into the valley. The angels drew the outlines of a city. When the bishop awoke, he was overwhelmed and convinced God had spoken to him.

He held a special Mass and went on a search for the valley of his dreams. When he saw a basin west of Mexico City, he recognized the area. He named it Puebla de los Angelos, or Home of the Angels.

The Spanish planned and built the little city, full of ornate buildings and historic homes. The city prospered with textiles and artisan pottery. For the last few decades, with a large population of Germans, it hosted the Volkswagen factory that made the popular Beetle. However, Pueblo had many economic setbacks and the people suffered the fate of all poor. Barely making enough to get by, many of Pueblo's males immigrated to the USA. In search of a better life, they worked in the underground economy of the United States, sending money home to support their families.

Manuel, her husband of ten years, was one of those men. Manuel had inherited a small farm from his family on the outskirts of Pueblo. However, it became impossible for him to scratch a living from the land. The cheap import of Canadian and American vegetables made his produce unsellable. He searched for work in the city, but for every job there were 100 men in line. When things got too tight, he had no choice. Like so many others, he crossed the border in search of work.

For the first month, Manuel was consistent. He sent a letter and money home each week. Then it ended. There was no word, no money, and no news from him. Maria knew he had been working in a suburban town in New Jersey. She wrote frantically to everyone she knew in the area. She had other wives question their husbands who had immigrated to the same area. No one knew. Maria had a sinking feeling. Manuel was not the type to disappear. He was devoted to his family and especially his two sons. As each day passed, Maria grew more frantic. Each night she prayed to Our Lady of Guadalupe. She had a special devotion to Mary.

When Manuel's brothers didn't hear from him, Maria began to think that some evil had befallen him. She decided to take the trip to the Basilica of Our Lady of Guadalupe in Mexico City to pray. It was a two-hour trip by bus to make the 80-mile distance from Pueblo. It was a greater distance in culture for a woman who had never left her home city.

Maria's fear for Manuel was greater than her fear of leaving her safe environment. Her devotion to Mary, Our Lady of Guadalupe, was intense. Getting on the bus that would take her to Mexico City and the Basilica, Maria knew if anyone could give her an answer about her missing husband, it would be the Mother of Christ.

The appearance of Our Lady had sealed the Aztec Indians' devotion to the Mother of Jesus. In the six-year period following her appearance, 6,000,000 Aztecs converted to Christianity. The new world was still unexplored in 1531 and yet heaven touched the Americas.

A poor Aztec Indian named Juan Diego was walking through the Tepayac Hill country in central Mexico. Along the way, he encountered a beautiful woman who was surrounded with a glowing light. She spoke to him in his native tongue and identified herself as Mary, the Mother of Jesus. She told him to go to the local bishop and tell him that she desired a church to be built on the site where she was appearing.

Although fearful, Juan went to see the bishop. Bishop-elect Fray Juan de Zumarraga was cordial and invited the peasant to visit again, but made no promise to build the church. Disappointed with the bishop's response, Juan Diego returned to the place where he had first seen Mary and she appeared to him again. Juan begged Mary to find someone with more influence to carry her message. He told her that the bishop needed proof of her appearance.

Mary told Juan Diego to return to Tepayac Hill the next day and she would give him the proof the bishop needed. Juan returned the next day and Mary appeared to him again. She listened as he prayed to her in intercession for his dying Uncle. Mary told him not to worry.

As for the sign for the bishop, she instructed Juan to climb the hill. At the top, he found a field of roses. Roses did not grow in that particular season. As part of his peasant's garb, Juan wore a tilma, a cape-like garment. He collected the flowers using his tilma as a pouch to carry the roses to the bishop.

When the bishop asked to see the sign, Juan opened the tilma to reveal the roses. As the roses tumbled out, the bishop fell to his knees. It was not the roses that caused the bishop and his advisors to kneel. It was the image of Mary, which now appeared on the tilma, just as Juan had described her. To this day, the tilma hangs in the Basilica that was built to honor Mary. This peasant garment should have deteriorated by now, but still hangs undisturbed.

When Juan returned home, his uncle met him, cured of his illness. The tilma was examined in 1977 and, even with infrared photography and digital enhancement, the origin of this holy image remains a mystery. Neither painted nor drawn, it is a source of miracles.

Maria needed a miracle.

The Basilica of Our Lady of Guadalupe was a large square with both the ancient Basilica and a modern Basilica built in the 1970's. The older building now acted as a museum of all the miracles that Mary had performed to those who prayed for her intercession. The newer Basilica was round and the tilma was placed in bulletproof glass above the altar. It is visible from all aspects of the church, but the modern building had moving walks that carried worshippers past this relic for a better view.

Maria rode the walkway a few times and the beauty of the image brought tears to her eyes. She settled in a pew to pray for the miracle she needed. *Mother Mary, help me find my Manuel. My boys need their father. Tell me what to do.* After praying the rosary and starting a novena, she rose from her now sore knees and stiffly hobbled toward the bus stop. She had not received an answer, but had faith that she would. The ride home was pleasant and Maria was glad to return to the mundane task of preparing dinner. In the back of her mind, she waited for the guidance she needed.

Her insight came that night as her prayer was answered in a dream. Maria dreamed she was walking down an avenue in a strange city. The people passing by spoke English and ignored her as they pushed past to their destinations. Maria held tightly to the hands of her sons who flanked both sides. In the dream, Maria was pregnant.

She searched the corners and stands of the city that she recognized as New York City. There on the streets, she saw Poblanoes selling flowers. Maria stopped and talked with many of her people, but no one had any news of Manuel. The boys were getting tired and cold and Maria's feet throbbed. She looked for a place for them to stay. Despite these troubles, Maria felt sure that she would find Manuel soon. Her heart was at peace.

When Maria awoke, she knew what she must do. She would take her boys and follow Manuel to the United States. It would not be easy. Falling to her knees beside her bed, she thanked the Blessed Mother for answering her prayers. Maria would go to America and find Manuel herself.

Telling her family was the hardest part. Her mother kept crying, "Maria, *no vaya!*" Her sisters and brothers begged, *"Es demasiado peligroso! Déle el tiempo – usted tendrá noticias de Manuel."* ("It is too dangerous! Give it time – you will hear from Manuel.") However, Maria had made up her mind. She sold all of her jewelry and some household items. After preparing for two weeks, she managed to raise *mil dólares* or $1,000.

The morning of their departure, Maria tried to hide her tears as her mother begged her not to go. The two boys were excited, thinking of the trip as a great adventure to find the father they missed. Boarding the bus, with small knapsacks of clothing and the money hidden in her bra, Maria scanned the home she loved so much. A sick feeling overcame her, a feeling that she would never see her mother or siblings again. She shook it off. Her prayer had been answered. She would follow the dream that Mary inspired. She would go to America and find her husband.

The bus took them to Altar, a small border town with a Catholic mission. *Coyotes* lined the road with vans and trucks. As they exited the bus, the coyotes (smugglers) called, "Come, for $2,000, I will get you to Boston." Another would try to outshout him, "For $700, I will get you to San Francisco." Maria kept the boys close as she bought supplies for the trip. She purchased two gallons of water, knowing they would be crossing the Sonoran Desert. She bought a small amount of food, but remained frugal.

She knew that most of her money would go to the *coyote* who would guide them into Arizona through the desert. Maria allowed the boys to take advantage of the cool drink and small snacks offered by the Catholic Hospitality house. She knew what they would face in the next few days would be brutal.

Going out into the afternoon sun, she made her way through the crowds of men making arrangements for crossing into the United States. Asking around, she found a *coyote* taking people toward New Jersey and the Mid-Atlantic states.

Pulling the boys by their hands, she pushed against the men, and reached the transporter. "My sons and I need to go to New Jersey."

Looking up, Juan, a rotund, middle-aged man laughed. "A thousand will do that."

Maria smiled, relieved. "I have a thousand."

Juan's eyes brightened. "A thousand each. Three thousand for you and your boys."

Maria felt crushed. "I only have a thousand, but they are such little boys and we would not take much space."

Juan laughed. "No ride for that. For that you need Jose. You'll be a walker."

After finding out where she could find Jose, Maria made arrangements to walk across the border.

"Meet me here at dusk. We will be walking through the desert all night and most of the day. When we reach Tucson, arrangements will be made for the trip to the Northeast."

Maria and her sons were the first waiting as the sun dipped low in the western sky. By the light of the full moon, the group, mainly consisting of young men, walked over the border into the desert. Maria pulled the black shawl around herself, despite the heat. She wanted to blend into the darkness to avoid any border patrols. The hard ground of the Sonoran Desert was hot and rough despite the night hours. During the day the temperature could reach 120 degrees; at night it remained an uncomfortable 98 degrees.

The boys grew tired after a few hours and their whining annoyed the men who were slowed by their short gait. *"Apresúrese! Usted nos hace más lentos!"* ("Hurry! You are slowing us down!") yelled Jose, as the men pushed ahead. The distance between Maria and the larger group grew greater. She struggled to keep up, but her feet throbbed with newly formed blisters and the boys clung to her, both tired and hungry. An elderly man with a large-brimmed, straw hat also slowed and seemed to be stressed. Worn out and weary they struggled on. Maria's feet swelled until her shoes felt like tourniquets, causing the blisters to open and, with new rubbing, they turned to blood blisters.

The sunrise doubled the agony. The warmth of the sun beat down on the sojourners and the black clothing they had worn to avoid the patrols absorbed the heat. The old man seemed confused. He started to wander away and the men who walked so far ahead paid no mind. Maria and the boys had used most of the water during the night and Maria was aware that she had not brought enough. Less than a pint remained and the day had just begun. She resolved that she would ration it as best as she could.

The old man talked nonsense and kept wandering as Maria repeatedly sent the boys to guide him back. Her head pounded as the sun beat down. Throbbing more than her feet, it made it hard for her to focus. As Maria looked ahead, the vestige seemed hazy, moving in waves that made no sense. The boys cried, whining for the little bit of water, crying to rest. Already the main group seemed further away. The men seemed to disappear over the horizon.

Again the elderly man stopped. This time instead of wandering, he collapsed. Sitting on the hard ground, he mumbled incoherently. Sitting beside him, Maria noticed his white, cracked lips. She recognized dehydration. Some of the men had not even brought water. Some of the younger men had reverted to drinking their own urine. Maria had tried to hang onto the small amount of water in her jug. Now she knew if she did not give it to the old man, he would die.

Looking at her boys, she sighed. She had no choice. Taking the jug from her knapsack, Maria begged, "Drink, drink the water." As she held the jug to the old man's lips, he drank greedily.

It seemed to revive him and suddenly he made sense as he talked. Standing with the strength the water gave him, he smiled. "Thank you, thank you. I will stay with you and help you. You have saved my life."

Maria wondered what the old man could do to help. Now all the water was gone and the day had just begun. They struggled ahead, aware of the growing distance between them and the main group. Maria felt weaker, her head pounding with the blazing sun. Her limbs ached as dehydration starved her muscles. Although she hadn't eaten in hours, she felt nauseous. Finally, unable to stand, she fell on her hands and knees and vomited. The copious vomit was bile that burned her throat and dehydrated her further. The old man helped her to her feet as the eyes of her two boys grew seriously frightened.

The second time she fell, it was the taste of the bile that made her nauseous. Vomiting again made her weaker and her head pounded. This time the old man seemed torn, unable to decide what to do. He looked from Maria and her boys, who tried to help her up, and the crowd of men who grew more distant.

In a split moment, he made his decision. "I'm sorry, I cannot wait for you. If I do I will die."

He turned toward the sun that was now high in the sky and strode quickly away. He never looked back. Maria rose again, with the help of her small sons, but knew their chances were slim.

Why did I give the last of our water to that man? she wondered as, in weakness, she walked even slower. However, the man would have died without the water and Maria knew that, under the same conditions, she would do the same thing.

Suddenly, Jose appeared, angry and agitated. He yelled, "We cannot wait for you. You are on your own."

"Do not leave us," Maria begged. "I paid a thousand dollars. We will die out here alone and without water."

Jose seemed to hesitate and then his face hardened with resolve. "Just keep walking. Do not give up. Keep the sun at your back. That way you know you are going to the east." He threw a bottle of water at her and went off, leaving the woman and her children behind.

Willing herself up, Maria took the bottle of water and shared some with the children. "Do not worry. Now that we have some water, we will finish the trip." The boys seemed reassured by her words. Tucking the water jug in her knapsack, Maria started off with a renewed courage.

With the sun to their backs, they walked for two hours, avoiding rattlers and some strange-looking lizards. Maria struggled to look strong, but as time went on, she became shaky and weak again. The sun's heat baked her mind. Stopping to rest and indulge in more drinks from the jug didn't help. She began vomiting uncontrollably and, as she lost control, Maria passed out.

When Maria awoke, a cold rag was over her head and Juan was sitting beside her. "Where is Roberto? Where is he?" The shaken woman sat up, holding the rag to her head.

Proud of his older brother, five-year-old Juan announced, "He went to get help. He just left."

Maria's heart leapt with fear. She had heard of so many who never made it through this final trip. Some drown in irrigation ditches or in the Rio Grande. Others died, baked in the desert. This was no place for a little boy. With renewed strength, she rose and took Juan's hand. Although still weak, she walked at a steady clip until she finally caught sight of Roberto. Calling out, she stayed him, allowing her to catch up to the determined child.

They walked silently for the next two hours, stopping only for sips from the jug. Maria could feel the sun baking her neck. Pain racked her joints and the nausea was back, causing occasional dry heaves. They were running low on water again and the sun grew hotter. Maria was afraid and feeling faint, and still she tried to push ahead. Her vision grew dull and she became dizzy. Just as she passed out, she saw the dirt road ahead.

When Maria awoke, she was on a gurney, in a cubicle in the ER, at the Medical Center in Tuscan. She had an IV dripping fluids into her dehydrated circulatory system. Her headache had disappeared.

Her two boys slept in plastic chairs at her bedside. She heard the beeps and blips of the machines around her. She heard the nurses talking outside the door.

"You have to call INS. This woman and her boys are Mexicans and they should be sent back. They clearly have no insurance and no money," a feminine voice stated.

"I'll make the call after I check the patient in cubicle two," answered another disembodied voice.

Maria aroused instantly, know exactly what she needed to do. Pulling out the IV, she dressed quickly. Awakening the boys, she held a finger to her lips. Scanning the hallway, she waited until it appeared empty and headed quickly to the sliding door. Exiting hastily she jogged through the parking lot and over to the next block.

Walking with both boys flanking her, Maria could only think about the next good step. She had suffered through the desert and it had landed her without money or a plan. She wasn't afraid; she knew the Blessed Mother was guiding her. In the dream Mary gave her, she had been pregnant. She hadn't understood it at the time, but now realized the truth. Maria was eight weeks pregnant when she crossed the desert. That had made the crossing more difficult.

Voices at play called Maria from her memories. *Yes, I toughed it out then, but what now? I'm just so tired,* she thought as she remembered her worries. *Blessed Mother, save me now,* she prayed. Rising she walked to the mail box. It had been two years, yet she had not found Manuel. There were times when she felt like giving up and going home. Only the dream kept her going, continuing the search.

Taking the mail to the table, she found the unmarked envelope and opened it with curiosity. When the hundred-dollar bill fell out she just stared at it. Then she began to cry. *Thank you Mary. Now I have enough for food.* The money was just enough to get them through and she was starting a new job as a full-time housekeeper for an older woman. Mrs. Hansen had a tough reputation, but Maria knew she would get along with her, whatever it took.

Maria was delighted at the periodical. She had often picked it up in a store or at church, but it had never been delivered. *What a treat.* Scanning the paper, she saw a story about a fire in the woods. A number of homeless men, mostly illegal aliens, lived in tent cities in the forest. In the winter, they used wood-burning stoves to heat the tents. One of the tents had caught fire during the night. No one had been hurt, but Maria sat in shock. There was a picture of the men huddled around an outside fire, struggling to keep warm.

Instantly, she recognized Manuel. Thin and emaciated, his clothes ragged and disheveled, he was living with other immigrants in a wooded area in this very town. Maria choked as tears flowed down her cheeks. She had found her Manuel because she received a paper she normally didn't get delivered. This was her miracle. Mary had answered all her prayers.

Maria sat in shock. She knew she had to grab her coat and the children, and head to the tent city where Manuel lived, but she couldn't move. She couldn't get over the miracle.

Eleven

"Stop judging, that you may not be judged. For as you judge, so will you be judged, and the measure with which you measure will be measured out to you." (Matt. 7:1-2)

Angie's small frame pulsed with emotion as her face reddened. Sister Val stood for a moment wondering how to put the child at ease. The petite woman decided that distraction was the best.

"Hate is a strange thing. You think it hurts the one you hate, but it usually hurts you more. I was born in a country full of hate. In my country, men hated each other for the different ideas each man had. The hate grew so large that men took guns, explosives, and chemicals to maim and kill the men who were different from themselves."

Angie continued to rant despite Sister Val's admonition, "Me get gun kill Tommy! No problem! Me kill 'im good and dead!"

Sister Val decided to take another approach and raised her voice slightly. "You should be ashamed of yourself. You don't deserve your name. Your name means angel, just like my name. Someone who hates and wants to kill is no angel."

Sister Val watched as Angie's eyes opened wide. The child sat back on the chair as if struck. Swallowing hard, she responded, "You right. Me no good to hate."

Turning her mind from her own troubles, she asked, "Sister Val mean angel?

The Asian woman tried to hide her pleasure at distracting the angry girl. "Sister Val is not my real name. Valerie is the name given to me when I came to this country. The parents who adopted me called me Valerie. My adoptive mother named me after her mother. My real name is Tien Ca' Le."

Angie seemed stunned. "Tien mean angel?"

"Yes," answered the woman, as she sent a young boy out to collect the bakery goods from Angie's bicycle.

"It's my Vietnamese name. I was born in the middle of hate. A war is an explosion of hate and killing. Because of hate, my father was killed and I was separated from my real mother. There were more than 2,000 babies flown over in military planes to this wonderful country and adopted. In 1975, when I was just an infant, I was put on a plane and flown to the United States. Some wonderful people adopted me. I don't think I'd be alive if I hadn't been saved. War and hate are terrible things."

Angie was shocked. "You away mother. No see like me. Me no mother, but Moma. You cry night?"

Tien Ca'Le looked carefully at the girl, now aware of their commonality. "When I was little, I cried. I always went somewhere alone to cry. I didn't want to hurt the parents who raised and loved me. I wanted to find my real mother. But I was lucky. A few years ago, I traveled back to Vietnam with other children who had come during Operation Baby Lift. I searched and found my mother. It was the greatest moment of my life."

Angie's mouth fell open in shock. "You find her! Me wish see mother. But she heaven. No can take plane to heaven."

"Yes," agreed Tien. Looking at the clock she knew it was time to serve the children. "Come, and let's get the lunch plated for the children. You can help me by making the sandwiches while I stir up the pitchers of lemonade."

Tien had started the community center years ago. Every Saturday, parents who worked would bring their children to be watched and cared for. It was an alternative to the danger and crime of the streets. Tien worked so hard to feed the children, who were from poor, working-class families.

Angie plated the cakes and buns she had carried from the bakery, reserving one coconut coffee cake for her last customer. She helped Tien make peanut butter and jelly sandwiches, then carried them out to the long table in the outer hall. In the gym, the children still played while lunch was prepared and the tables set. Sister Val had some older teenagers who watched the younger kids while she made lunch.

The community center was a large, ramshackle building that had been erected in the late sixties. The burner puttered on and off on any given day. In the heat of summer, there was no air conditioning. The roof leaked whenever it rained. There were no funds for repairs, but Sister Val carried on with complete dedication despite numerous complaints. She had dedicated her life to the community center and the needs of the children in this part of town.

When the lunch was served, fifty children of various ages came in from the gym and settled down to eat. Sister Val relaxed and sat close to Angie.

"How you find mother?" the girl asked.

A sense of supernatural awe came over Tien as she spoke in hushed tones. "It was truly a miracle. My adopted mother had a paper that came with me. My father's name and the fact that he was deceased were on the front of the paper. Strangely, on the back of the paper, written by hand, were a number of lines that no one could read. The words were written in Vietnamese and no one knew what it was until, as a college student, I had it translated.

It was a small prayer to Our Lady of La Vang, written and signed by my real mother. In the midst of war, she had no choice but to send me to a place where I would be safe. But she didn't send me off alone; she sent me with a prayer. It was this prayer that helped me to find her."

"Who be the lady?" Angie asked.

Tien, pulled from her musings, explained, "The Lady of La Vang is the Blessed Mother, the Mother of Jesus. Even many centuries ago, there was hate. People hated Christians and hunted them down to kill them. The Christians in Vietnam had to hide and went into the jungle to escape their persecutors. They hid in Quang Tri, a village in the center of Vietnam. There they were safe, but they were hungry, and many became ill.

Thinking they were going to die, they came together to pray. As they prayed, shining lights surrounding them and a beautiful lady appeared. She told them she was the Mother of God and comforted them. In the jungle there was a special fern that grew. The woman told them to use the leaves of the fern to treat all their ailments. She told them their prayers would be answered. The Blessed Lady appeared to them many times to give them courage and the leaves healed them."

"Wow, she be Mary!" announced Angie as her eyes opened wide.

"Yes," answered Tien as she poured some lemonade for the children coming up for seconds. "She returned 100 years later when the Christians were again being killed. So many Christians, 100,000 Vietnamese Christians, were martyred for their faith. Men can hate so much. The people remembered the visits of the Lady and so they built a church on the spot where she appeared. They called her Our Lady of La Vang, which means Our Lady of the Fern. Now there is a big basilica for all the people to visit. The poem my mother wrote made me go there. And it was there, I found my mother."

Angie remained speechless, as a tear rolled down Tien's cheek. Tien felt so moved by the miracle of finding her mother that she ignored the present. Angie's question called her back.

"You mother sit church years for you read poem?" asked the girl.

Tien tilted her head as she deciphered the question and then started to laugh. "No Angie, she didn't sit in the church for years waiting. The miracle was that she was so devoted to Our Lady of La Vang that she took a job as the housekeeper in the rectory of the church. She worked there for all those years. When I came into the church, I knelt down to pray. I noticed the cleaning woman as she was sweeping the aisle of the church. When I pulled out the paper with the prayer, the cleaning woman started to scream and fell to her knees. She was my mother and recognized the paper immediately. The prayer she had written had brought her baby girl home to her."

There was a moment of silence before Angie responded, "Mary be so good. Angie bad. Angie hate. This be sin. No hate Tommy. Tommy be bad. But Angie not bad."

Tien smiled. "Now you understand. There are always bad men, men full of hate. But we belong to Our Lady. She teaches us how to love. Now, no more talk of hate. We need to get the cakes out on the tables."

Angie helped distribute the desserts, delighting the children. It was rare that they got treats, but each week Angie's gifts sweetened their lunch. When she was done, she sat back beside Sister Val or, as she knew her now, Tien.

One of the older boys came up to the table with a grim look. "Sister Val, the faucet in the kitchen is giving dark, muddy water again. I can't make drinks for the children.

Color rose in Tien's face. "This place is falling apart and no one cares. The well needs replacing, the pipes are leaking. No one cares about these children, no one but me."

Angie watched as anger rose to color the tiny woman's cheeks. "You be happy. Now you sad. You forget mother?"

Tien, distracted from her resentment, looked at the child. "No, I thank Our Lady of La Vang for finding my mother each day, but this place needs so much work. No one cares and no one helps."

Tilting her head quizzically the girl answered, "No one help 'cause you no ask."

Tien was shocked. "What do you mean, I don't ask?"

Angie answered, "Who you ask help. You no ask. You think only you good. No think good anyone else. You no ask help."

Tien shook her head. "Who should I ask? Nobody cares about my children, except me. I work night and day, never stopping to take care of myself. No one else worries about my children."

Angie laughed. "No your children. They God's children. You no ask. You selfish."

Tien's face grew scarlet. "How can you say that? I love these children."

"Yes, but keep love all self. Ask help God's children. Lot's love and help. Who that?" the young girl pointed to the end of the cafeteria. All of the children had left, but one sandy-haired boy sat alone in a wheelchair.

Looking down to the end of the table, Tien answered, "Oh, that's Logan, one of our foster children. He's new. I better get someone to take him out."

"He no walk?" asked Angie.

"There's no reason physically. He is just non-responsive since he was taken from his mother."

The girl looked confused and Tien realized the simple mind she had addressed, "I mean Logan doesn't walk or talk. He isn't sick, but he is so sad at being taken away from his mother, that he won't do anything. His mother had to go to jail and he's with a foster family. He hasn't talked since they took her away."

"Me bring outside," offered Angie as she headed toward the boy.

Tien headed to the problems in the kitchen. She was determined to fix the plumbing, but her mind kept running over the child's words. Selfish? Am I selfish? Tien couldn't fathom what the girl had said, yet it ran through her mind as she drained the kitchen pipes. *I would take help, wouldn't I?* Yet she had to admit that she had never really asked for help. Why she hadn't was beyond her.

As the water began to run clear again, it struck her. *Why was she judging others so harshly? Why wouldn't she ask for help?* Tien looked at her own behavior with new eyes. *Who would believe such a simple child could see so deeply?*

Twelve

When Jesus saw his mother and the disciple there whom he loved, he said to his mother, "Woman, behold your son." Then he said to the disciple, "Behold, your mother." And from that hour the disciple took her into his home (John 19:26-27)

Everyone suffers because suffering is a part of this life. My Grandmother always thought that the purgatory we experience happens in this life, and the hell of it was that we didn't understand it. Some suffering is sudden and unexpected, as when an accident impacts our body. Unprepared, we go into shock as the body that always carried us now betrays us. With blessing it is a temporary awakening to our fragility. In some cases it is a life-altering experience. Emotional anguish can cause tears and regret as a friendship or relationship ends.

How we recuperate from the blows of life defines us. Our coping depends greatly on our belief system and the strength of our inner spirit. Emotional, spiritual, mental or physical suffering can be acute or chronic, carried with depression or a wise resignation. However, the worst kind of suffering has our deepest fear attached to it. Our greatest suffering is when our fear becomes our truth.

Logan always feared that his mother would leave and not return. He had nightmares of her going out to buy the drugs she craved, only to fall victim to the dangers of the night. Sometimes he would lie awake, terrorized by the lusting faces of the men who took his mother out. His mother sold her body to fill the emptiness that only crack-cocaine seemed to fill. The chubby boy dreamed of being enough, enough to heal the endless wound in his mother's heart. He dreamed of a day when his love would be sufficient to mend her soul. His nightmares told him that he never would.

Lying in his bed in the dim light of their apartment, another kind of darkness entered his heart. The oppressive fear of her never returning crushed him. He couldn't sleep until he heard her key unlocking the door. Sometimes, he had time to catch a few hours of sleep before school. Other times he was already making breakfast, hoping to nourish her thin body. Then, on one anticipated morning, his fear became reality. She left, disappearing into the shadows of the night and didn't return with the sunrise. Logan stayed home from school, too anxious to settle down. He kept busy – trying to tap the overwhelming anxiety that quickened his heart. He was cleaning the counter, a counter he already wiped three times, when Child Services arrived.

Logan's heart leapt with joy when he heard the knock on the door. Somewhere his mind refused to pose the question of why his mother would knock. She had a key. However, as the seven-year-old unlocked the deadbolt and the nicked metal door swung open, his mind registered the fact that it wasn't good news. Standing at the door, an elderly, frail woman carried a briefcase and was dressed in an official-looking, brown suit. A policeman stood behind her giving authority to her small frame. Logan's body almost collapsed with the overwhelming sense of dread.

Stepping inside, the woman looked around the barely furnished rooms. "Hello son. Is anyone here with you?" Logan's heart sank as he realized the gravity of her discovery.

"My mommy just ran out to a neighbor's. She'll be back right away," answered the boy.

The woman from the state showed no emotion as she opened the empty refrigerator and scanned the empty cabinets in the kitchen. "Have you eaten today?" Logan froze, unable to answer. His alarm was well founded and, as the truth unraveled itself, Logan's body locked his mind away from the pain.

His mother had been caught trying to buy drugs from an undercover cop. There was a bail that no one would pay so she would sit in jail until her trial. She would be appointed a lawyer who would half-heartedly fight for a reduced sentence. Logan knew the truth. He had classmates, fellow sojourners of the downtrodden neighborhood, whose mothers had been caught doing or selling drugs. He would be grown by the time she was paroled. As the fear of what faced him came to light, Logan withdrew from reality.

In the darkness of his fear, the boy regressed into the only safe place he knew – himself. Over the coming weeks, he slowly stopped talking or even walking. He lived in a world none could enter. Numerous doctors could find nothing physically wrong with the boy. Against advice, the social worker took a gamble and placed him in a foster home with kind and experienced caretakers, hoping in time he would rejoin the world. However, Logan remained in the darkness. If he didn't engage the real world soon, he would be placed in an institution for the emotionally ill. If he didn't come out of his catatonic state, the world would leave him behind.

Angie watched as everyone left the cafeteria, leaving just her and the boy alone. She crossed the room quickly, sitting next to him. He didn't acknowledge her and continued to stare straight ahead.

"What you name?" asked the girl as she tilted her head curiously. Logan didn't move.

"Why you no say nothing?" she asked. Still there was no response from the boy.

"You no walk?" Angie tried again to will movement from the

boy.

Angie turned red with anger. "Why you mean, so mean to me? You be like Tommy. He be mean and call names. But he look me. You so mean. You no look." Still there was no reaction from the boy.

Angie shifted side-to-side in her chair as she grew agitated. "No you mouth work?"

She started to poke her pointer finger, touching Logan's lips. "No you mouth work?" she repeated in a sing-song verse as she continued to poke at the compressed lips. Jabbing continuously Angie continued her song. "No you mouth work? No you mouth work?" She tried to pry his mouth open with her finger. Logan compressed his mouth tighter and his face reddened as he turned away from Angie's probing fingers. She laughed. "See! You move."

Slipping off her chair, she sat on the floor in front of Logan's wheelchair. She grasped both of his ankles with her hands and, lifting up each leg alternately; she began another sing-song. "Look you be walking. Look you be walking." Angie laughed as she quickened the pace. "Look you be running. Look you be running."

The angry boy started to squirm. Angie was having too much fun to notice and started to move with rhythm, continuing to laugh. "Look you be dancing!" She didn't notice the glare of pure hatred that the boy leveled at her.

Jumping to her feet, Angie took both her thumbs and pointer fingers and grasped the boy's lips. "Look you be talking! You be singing!"

Without warning, Logan jumped to his feet. The force knocked the wheelchair backward. "Leave me alone!"

The shout was so loud, it startled Angie. It took an instant for her to recover from the shock and then she was overjoyed.

"You be walking and be talking," exclaimed the happy girl. She clapped her hands and danced around in front of Logan.

"Why couldn't you leave me alone!" he shouted.

The noise drew Tien and her help from the kitchen. When they witnessed Logan standing and shouting, the kitchen helpers started toward the scene. Tien reached out her arm and held them back. The teenagers straggled in from the gym, intent on finding the source of the noise, Tien held up her hand to indicate they should not intervene.

As Angie danced in front of him, Logan shouted, "Why didn't you just leave me alone? Get out of here and leave me alone!"

Angie stopped dancing and placed her hand on her hip. "You no be alone. Moma say no good be alone. You be with Angie. Be friend to Angie."

Logan started to cry. "You don't know about me. My mommy is gone. I don't want to talk or walk or even be here without her."

Angie reached out to the boy and took him in her arms. "You be so scared. Too scared walk or talk. No be scared alone. Better be scared with friend."

Logan didn't respond because he didn't hear her. He only heard the roaring flood of emotions that had been dammed up within him. The boy's sobs overcame him and his small body shook. He folded his arms and laid his head down on the table.

Loudly he sobbed, "I want my Mommy!"

Angie stood watching as the pain of his loss overwhelmed him. Out loud she asked, as if asking the universe, "What me do?" She walked toward the boy. Embracing him, Angie whispered, "Miss Mommy too. When miss Mommy, Moma say get up on lap and cry. You come, come my lap and cry."

She sat beside Logan and positioned herself to receive him. Opening her arms, she drew him onto her lap. Logan clung to her, laying his head on her small shoulder. His weeping grew deeper as he held tightly to Angie. The girl said nothing, but simply held the boy until his cries grew softer and subsided. As Logan cried himself out, all the pain bound in his frozen heart and body was released.

Tien watched the scene play out before her. A smile kissed her face as she understood the healing that was taking place. If Logan had to release all his hurt and terror, God had provided just the person to receive it, thought Tien. As the boy's weeping subsided,

Angie allowed him to take the lead and, as he gently pulled away, she looked at him tenderly.

"Better now rest," Angie whispered as the boy stopped crying, "Mommy be away now. But not always."

"I have no one now," whispered Logan in a forlorn tone.

Angie looked thoughtful for a few moments, and then her face lit up with an idea. Tien listened with delight as Angie told Tien's story of finding her lost mother. Of course, the story had all the embellishments of Angie's imagination. The Lady of the Fern became the Lady of the Magic Tree. Angels sang and danced in the sky as the Lady appeared on a mountain in England. Tien had to cover her mouth with her hand. She didn't want to laugh out loud as knights and King Arthur became part of the story. In the end, there was a big parade where Tien and her mother sat on thrones on a golden float. Logan was hypnotized with interest.

Winding up, Angie announced with pure faith, "So you see mother again. And there be big celebration."

Logan seemed content about the future, but worried about the present. "But who will be my mother now? Who will talk to me and listen to me? Who will watch over me when I'm sick?"

Angie stroked the young boy's head, pausing before she answered. Tien realized the girl was having a conversation with someone else, someone in her heart.

Angie didn't want to give up the beautiful card Father Hogan had given her. The picture of the Blessed Mother was so colorful and peaceful. *Me no have mother either. Why me can no look at the picture when me want a mother?* Angie silently replied to the prompting in her heart. With a sigh, she surrendered. Taking the card from her back hip pocket, Angie looked longingly at the face of Mary who held the Christ child gently in her arms. Angie loved the picture, but she knew what she had to do.

"Logan. Here you mother. She Jesus' mother. She be you mother now. You talk her and look her." Angie gave up the lovely image of Mary.

Logan took the card respectfully and whispered, "Wow, she's beautiful. I'll take good care of her."

"She take good care you." Angie pushed Logan off her lap and onto his feet. "Gotta go now. One paper to give."

Tien approached. "Angie, maybe you should just go home now. It's late and you do have a lot of cuts and scrapes."

"No, no." Angie got excited. "One more paper. Gotta go!"

Tien could see the girl was becoming overwrought at the thought of missing her last delivery. "Okay, Angie, go and deliver your paper. Hurry up and then go right home. Watch out for that boy and be very careful."

"Me go now," Angie insisted as she left through the kitchen door toward her bike. She was anxious to go, excited to see her last customer.

As Angie took off on her bike, Mrs. Lennon was just pulling into the center. Parking her car, she called after the girl, but Angie was out of earshot. Walking to the center's kitchen door with her trays of cookies, she was met by Sister Val, who had been watching the girl leave.

"I wish she would just go home. She was pretty scraped up by that boy's attack," Sister Val told Mrs. Lennon.

Putting the trays of cookies on the counter, Mrs. Lennon asked, "What attack?"

The small Asian woman graphically explained the encounter Angie had experienced in the park. Mrs. Lennon got a sickly feeling in her gut. When she heard about the cuts and scrapes Angie had sustained, a sense of dread overtook her.

Val ended her story by adding, "I warned her not to go through the park again, but you know Angie. She'll probably take the quickest way. That boy is probably long gone anyway." Val ended her attention to the child's problems by thanking Mrs. Lennon profusely for the cookies, "The children will love these. What made you think of the needs of the center?"

Distracted, Mrs. Lennon murmured, "Oh Angie was by delivering the paper. She mentioned the children and I just thought they would enjoy the cookies."

Val continued the conversation while preparing the treat by plating the delectable donation. To Mrs. Lennon, the other woman's words were just a drone as her mind was on Angie. She couldn't shake the feeling of impending danger. Reaching for the cell phone in her pocket, Mrs. Lennon dialed Moma's number.

Josh had just entered the kitchen, home from a victorious ball game, when the phone rang. Picking up the receiver, his voice registered surprise upon hearing Mrs. Lennon.

"Hi, Josh, is that you?" she asked. "Listen, I'm worried about Angie." Explaining the rock-throwing incident, she suggested Josh should come and walk Angie home safely.

In a concerned tone he answered, "Don't worry, I'll come and get Angie and I'll swing through the park just to make sure Tommy's not still there."

"Oh great, Josh. I'd feel much better if you did."

Clicking off the phone, the woman realized the lie of her statement. She couldn't shake the feeling of trepidation that consumed her.

Thirteen

And when he had said this, he breathed on them and said to them, "Receive the holy Spirit. Whose sins you forgive are forgiven them, and whose sins you retain are retained." (John 20:22)

There are times when we dream of running away. It is a common fantasy. We can leave our past, our burdens, and our sorrows behind. What would happen if we just got on a bus or a train and went somewhere, anywhere, to an unfamiliar place? We could give ourselves a new name – one we like better. We could find a job, a different job, one with less pressure, or our dream job. All those people who abuse, hurt, or restrain us would wonder where we went Wouldn't it serve them right? They never appreciated us anyway. Maybe we would be wiser in the new life. Maybe we could just start over and avoid all the mistakes that defined our old life.

We waste away a lazy afternoon imagining where we would go or what we would do, but most of us never indulge this fantasy. When the daydreaming ends, we return to our real life, the life with the mundane burdens, and expected responsibilities. Why? Because we are aware of the true cost of running away and we know the cost is too high. The cost is unfulfilled relationships and haunting memories. The true fee of our imagined freedom is years of wonder and regret as we mourn an unfinished life. Deep inside we know our life is a story, one that we created, and it is up to us to finish that story.

Yet, some of us indulge the fantasy. Millions of people are listed on the roles of missing persons. Many are absent by their own hand.

Angie knew such a person and she was headed to see him now. She always saved a coconut coffee cake for Mr. Arthur. It was his favorite and she loved to see him smile. He lived in a dilapidated bungalow in the poorest section in town. A rusted, chain link fence surrounded the home of peeling paint and weeds. The house was as ugly as the poverty that created it. At one time it had been a beautiful home, someone's dream. Like Mr. Arthur's life, it had changed. Without care, all things die.

Climbing cautiously off her bike, Angie was aware of how painful her scraped knees felt. The sight of George, Mr. Arthur's black Labrador retriever, made her forget the pain. George was supposed to be a watchdog, carefully guarding the meager possessions of the man of the house. He usually barked loudly, frightening passersby. He never barked at Angie because he loved her. Angie had always wanted a dog of her own, but Moma thought it would be too much work and responsibility. If ever she was to have a dog, it would be George. He met her at the gate and, jumping up, licked her face with unbounded joy.

Angie giggled, but as she opened the gate, she put on an extremely serious face. She didn't want George to run out of the gateway as he had that one time. That day, he had disappeared so quickly that neither Mr. Arthur nor Angie could find him. He got in a lot of trouble and terrorized all the people around the block at the run-down market. Apparently, one woman was so afraid of the large dog, she dropped her brown bag of groceries, breaking all the eggs and the jug of milk she had just purchased. George enjoyed the free treat. Mr. Arthur ended up using what little money he had to pay for the eggs and milk. They finally managed to capture George right before the animal control people arrived. Angie was relieved. *George end up jail. Bad boy*, thought Angie, as she carefully squeezed through the slightly opened gate.

"Sit, sit!" commanded Angie and the large dog jumped a few more times. Finally, he followed her command, with his tongue hanging, awaiting the customary treat Angie had in her pocket. He was not disappointed. She took out the biscuit and tossed it up in the air. George caught it cleanly and made short order of the treat.

"Be good dog, stay!" Angie ordered as she stood pointing her finger. George tried, but only for a moment. He couldn't resist showing his enthusiasm for the girl and, within moments, he was bouncing up and down like a top. Angie laughed at his joy. She heard laughter behind her and turned to see Mr. Arthur on the porch. He had been there watching all along.

Mr. Arthur was a thin man. His chiseled face held a week's worth of stubble and his worn and pilled, brown sweater was his daily uniform. Mr. Arthur was the poorest man Angie knew. His refrigerator held scant amounts of food. His cupboards were usually bare, except for a collection of loose tea bags, a box of stale crackers, and soup tins. It seemed to Angie that Mr. Arthur survived on Campbell's soup. His shelves were lined with dozens of cans of tomato, chicken noodle, and vegetable soups. He waited for the can-can sales at the market where George had his troubles.

Mr. Arthur supplemented his supply with the valued treasures from the pantry at the church on the corner. Zion AME Baptist was a white, clapboard church with a tall, narrow steeple. On Wednesdays, they gave out bags of groceries to the needy, which had been donated by numerous merchants in the area. There was usually a long line for the goods.

In the winter, Mr. Arthur made good use of an ancient, wood-burning stove in the kitchen of his home although wood was not the only thing he burned for heat. Summers were spent on the porch, cooled by a small, rotating fan found in someone's trash. How he survived without any known source of income was anyone's guess. Angie never understood the level of poverty that plagued most of this neighborhood. It was not part of her world. She only knew that the coconut cake she brought was the highlight of Mr. Arthur's week. What he failed to understand was spending time with him was the best part of Angie's week.

"How you be?" asked Angie as she walked up the rickety steps to the worn, wooden porch that spanned the front of the bungalow. George followed on her heels and laid his massive head across her feet as she sat in the plastic lawn chair.

"No complaints," he answered as he rose to enter the house. "I'll make us some tea to go with our cake."

Angie stayed on the porch and waited. She had gotten here late today and hoped it didn't mean less time with George and Mr. Arthur.

Cutting generous portions of the cake, Angie gave a piece to George as his owner carried two mugs of steaming tea and set them on the wobbly, round table.

"Angie, where did you hurt yourself?" asked the man as he noticed all the bandages the girl sported. Angie spent half an hour giving a blow-by-blow description of her encounter in the park.

Dunking his cake in his tea, Mr. Arthur listened quietly. He was not much of a talker, usually allowing Angie to take the lead, while he sat listening. It bothered Angie that he didn't talk much. There was so much she wanted to ask him, but she tried hard to keep her questions inside. Each week she would pose a different query, in a nonchalant way, so as not to cause him fear. Angie knew somewhere deep in her spirit that if she frightened Mr. Arthur, he would just retreat. That was the last thing she wanted. She was very gentle with her inquiries.

This approach, although just an instinct for Angie, seemed to work. It was a slow process, but she was so afraid Mr. Arthur would run away or lock his door to an obvious interrogation. They sipped their tea, had second pieces of the coconut cake, and bantered on about the news before Angie got up the nerve to tap her curiosity.

"You be alone, all the time?" she broached.

Mr. Arthur's eyes took on a pained look. "Yes, I live all alone.

"You friends?" Angie asked as calmly as she could.

"No, not really, except for your visits, I pretty much keep to myself. I talk to the woman who runs the pantry down at the church. Oh, and, of course, there's George."

At the mention of his name, the black lab lifted his head, but seeing he was not being offered more cake, rested his jowls on Angie's sneakers.

The small girl took a sip of the hot tea as she tried to get up the courage for her next question. "Why name George?"

Mr. Arthur smiled and, with a faraway look in his eyes, answered, "Did you ever see the movie, *It's a Wonderful Life?*"

Angie tried hard to remember, but finally shook her head.

Mr. Arthur responded, "It's a favorite around the holidays. It's about a man who wishes he'd never been born. An angel shows him what the world would have been like if he hadn't been born. Things in his town turn out terrible without him living there. Anyway, the main character is named George Bailey. When he does get back to his town, he runs like a maniac, looking for the people he loves. When I saw George as a puppy, he ran around so excited and was so jumpy, he reminded me of George Bailey. That's how he got the name George."

Angie petted George's brow, afraid to look at Mr. Arthur as she asked the question, afraid she might cry. "Do you have a family?"

"I had a family once. I don't have one anymore," he answered wistfully.

Angie gulped hard. She knew she was taking a risk, but just had to pose her next question, "You family dead?"

There was a silent moment, an extended pause. The child looked up, nervously, expecting to see anger. Instead, she saw tears.

"No I'm the one who's dead. My family is still alive, but not for me. They hate me and want nothing to do with me," he whispered.

"You no dead – go tell 'em," Angie said.

Mr. Arthur remained silent and just stared at Angie. *Oh no,* thought Angie, *Me say too much. He mad now.* She watched his face and the emotions that passed over it. She was relieved when he stopped staring and looked toward the street, with that pensive way he always had.

"Did you ever do anything bad?" he asked as he turned to the quizzical girl.

"Oh yeah, me do lots bad. Try be good but no can help," she answered.

"What do you do when you realize you did something bad?" the man asked.

"Me sorry, ask forgive," she explained.

"Sometimes, a person does something so bad they can't be forgiven. There's no way to make it better," Mr. Arthur answered with a faraway look in his eyes. "What's the worst thing you've ever done?"

Angie scrunched her face hard as she thought. Reaching into the past, she pulled up the biggest shame she had. "Once me take Moma's favorite necklace. It be white, round stones, so smooth. Me wear playing. It break. No can fix so bury in dirt. Me no tell. She cries. It be gift from Mommy to her. Me know she hurt. So Angie run away."

Mr. Arthur seemed interested. "What made you go home?"

"Angie's feet hurt. Me walk and walk. Get so tired. House look so good," the girl stated.

"What do you mean, the house looked good? How could you see it if you walked so far?" he asked.

"Oh, me walk around, around. No allowed cross street," she explained.

Mr. Arthur paused for a moment and then smiled. "You mean that you walked around the block, over and over, because you weren't allowed to cross the street."

"Yeah, me be so tired. Feet hurt," answered the girl, exasperated as she thought of her dilemma. "First, me look house. See Moma cook. Me belly growl. Next me look. See Moma clean alone. No Angie help. Then me look. See Moma sit alone. Me go home."

"How did you go home?" asked Mr. Arthur.

"I go, tell truth. Be sorry. Moma hug, forgive. What you do so bad?"

Mr. Arthur sighed. "My bad thing was running away. I ran away when my family needed me most. I was afraid of taking care of everyone. I panicked and ran. Maybe if I wasn't allowed to cross the street, things would have been better. However, I was an adult and I just kept running. One day became a week, weeks turned to months. Now it's been years and there's no going back. There's no hug or forgiveness for me."

Angie watched as Mr. Arthur struggled to suppress a sob. She could feel her heart breaking, a sore spot in the middle of her chest. She felt her eyes filling with tears. *Me so stupid. No words be right. Jesus help me. Give me right words,* Angie prayed.

"You go home. They forgive and hug," Angie whispered as she looked the other way to hide her pain.

"No, Angie, there's no forgiveness for me. What I did was too bad," the man sighed.

"Jesus forgive. Forgive even men who kill him. He forgive you," Angie begged.

Mr. Arthur rose, rubbing both hands along his thighs as if to wipe away the pain. "Maybe Jesus can forgive, but my family never will. Why should they? I wouldn't."

Angie got up and started down the porch steps. She knew if she stayed a minute longer, she would burst into tears. "You wrong. Family forgive. You no forgive self. Gotta go, late."

She looked back as she climbed on her bike. Mr. Arthur appeared forlorn as George jumped up and down in longing for his little friend. Angie had said too much. She had to pedal and get away quickly. Mr. Arthur didn't know who he was, but Angie did. She had seen his photo in Moma's picture album.

Fourteen

"Behold, I am laying a stone in Zion that will make people stumble and a rock that will make them fall, and whoever believes in him shall not be put to shame. (Rom. 9:33)

Furious, Josh slammed the phone. "I'll beat the life out of that kid!" he whispered to himself. Angie was so defenseless. *Why can't that kid just leave her alone?* He unhooked his cell phone from the charger and shoved it in his pocket. He wrote a note for Moma, telling her where he had gone. She was visiting a sick neighbor with a gift of one of her casseroles. *A good beating will teach that Tommy,* he decided as he put on his jacket and pulled his bike from the garage.

His anger boiled as he thought of the cuts and scrapes Mrs. Lennon had described on the phone. He would like to wipe the street with that brat. Still, he knew in his heart, he'd never beat a younger and smaller boy so Josh decided he would just scare him. He would scare him a lot. If Tommy were frightened of what Josh would do, he might leave Angie alone.

Josh knew Angie's route, but didn't have any idea where she might be. The route would take a normal person about an hour to ride, but his sister had her own way. She would visit people along the way, staying longer with different customers on various weeks. She could go straight in a logical way, but she usually meandered in a zigzag pattern according to her whim. She was even known to visit customers that she alone knew. People she gave papers to, who weren't on the printed route. Sometimes it took her all day to deliver the free news.

Josh was worried about Angie, worried about where she might be if she were emotionally distraught. He would have to ride around until he ran into her. In the meantime, he might run into Tommy. Josh decided he would make short order of dealing with that bully. *Well, at least I know Angie will stay away from the park. I doubt that Tommy is still there anyway.* He mounted his bike and headed out to town.

She had held her emotions inside as she sat on that run-down porch. She couldn't look at Mr. Arthur when he was sad. She just wanted to run to him and hold him in her arms. She wanted to tell him who she was and that she loved him.

Angie could feel the hot tears on her cheeks and had to stop riding as her vision blurred. The bike shook as she gripped it. Standing alone at the corner, she sobbed heavily, allowing all her pent-up feelings out.

Angie wanted to tell him it was all right; his family did forgive him and wanted him to come home. In fact they needed him to come home. Yet, when she looked in his eyes and saw the deep pain, the faraway look, she knew she shouldn't tell him. She never did. Angie knew deep in her soul, that such a move would scare him away.

Mr. Arthur had been away long enough. She wanted him to come home. And now she wanted nothing more than to be home herself. Looking up, she could see the sun was low in the winter sky. In a few hours it would be dark. She just wanted to be home, to feel Moma's arms around her.

Angie knew she had a choice – she could ride along the tracks and take the lengthy way home or she could cut through the park. For a minute she vacillated, but making her decision out of emotion, Angie ignored the warning in her heart. She headed toward the park. She just wanted to get home. *Tommy probably gone*, she decided.

The wind, warm for a winter day, blew gently. The speed of

Angie's bike thrilled her, so different from her slow, measured everyday pace. The ride seemed to calm her. Angie thought about what she needed to do.

Angie's thoughts moved at a slower pace than everyone else. What took others just a few minutes to reason out, took her much longer, but this didn't bother her. As long as she could come to sound conclusions, she was satisfied with the process. Her slowness did seem to bother other people, but as Moma always said, "What bothers others is their concern, not yours."

It took three times as long to decide her next course of action, but Angie made up her mind. It wouldn't help for Mr. Arthur to discover who she was. When she visited him next Saturday, she would be more careful. Angie wiped the tears from her cheeks as she traveled. *Me need be careful. He be so afraid. Be gone if he know*, she thought as she puzzled over how she should act around Mr. Arthur.

Riding past the Community Center, as she made a turn for the park entrance, she noticed Mrs. Lennon's car. Oh good. She bring cookie. Angie thought of stopping to see Mrs. Lennon and asking for one of the cookies. She thought that having a cookie with Logan, her new friend might be nice. However, she was so late, she decided to just head for home.

At the entrance to the park, Angie stopped. She knew she was late, but the ground was full of pine cones. Angie was easily distracted, especially by fond memories. Moma loved to make things with pine cones. Angie spent every November helping Moma make all the beautiful pine-cone wreaths that she gave as gifts each year.

They would sit at the kitchen table, while Angie soaked the cones. Wet and pliable, Moma would weave the cones through a rounded wire, taking care that each cone covered the circular wire form at different angles. When she was done, they would let the wreaths dry and then hot-glue ribbons and decorations to each one. Sometimes they spray-painted the cones with white paint, making them look as if snow had fallen on them. No two wreaths were the same and giving out the wreaths was one of Angie's favorite parts of

Christmas.

Now that the weather had been warm, the cones that had been buried in the snow were visible. Angie collected all the best pine cones under the grove of evergreens that stood before the entrance to the park. Moma would store them until they made the wreaths next fall. She filled her basket, anxious to get home and share her find with Moma.

Retracing the very route that had been her escape just a short time ago, she turned off the asphalt and rode the gravel path into the park. The dust from the rocks kicked up a cloud as she pedaled along. She grew just a little afraid when she reached the part of the roadway where she had run into Tommy earlier. She wondered if it had been smart to take such a chance. It was too late to change her direction now. Looking around, she didn't see anyone. Taking a deep breath, she peddled faster and, as she continued, started to feel safe in her choice. Then, much to Angie's shock, Tommy jumped out on the path just 20 feet ahead.

Angie applied the brakes, creating a spray of gravel as her bike came to a screeching halt just ten feet from the boy. Tommy stood blocking the road. *Me turn round and run fast*, she thought, knowing she was too close to the boy to get away. For the first time in her life, Angie froze. She looked around, unable to see a way out of her quandary. He didn't run toward her or try to grab her. He just stood there, staring at her, and somehow his immobility terrified her more. It was eerie, him just standing there. He didn't move a muscle. Unable to decide where to go or what to do, Angie remained, staring back at her enemy.

Tommy could feel the spirits swirl around him. They were the ones who told him to wait for her return. Now they whispered deep and low to his spirit.

Oh, now you have her. Don't be stupid. Don't let her get away, urged the smallest dark entity.

No one will know. Kill her and she'll never make you feel like a moron with those dumb poems again, cried the Spirit of Murder.

The wounded boy believed their whispers were his own thoughts. The thoughts made him feel smart. They gave him a sense of pride, of being one up on everyone else. Congratulating himself on cornering her, he decided to take note of the voices. He would try a new approach with Angie.

"Don't be afraid. I'm not going to hurt you," he shouted.

"I know you. You bad. Hurt me," Angie whined.

"No, I'm sorry for throwing the rock. I just want to see if you're all right," he answered.

Angie looked confused. Tommy had put on a different persona. *I've got to look like I'm sorry,* he thought. He tried not to laugh as he watched her hands shake.

"You hate Angie. Always. You be mean," accused Angie

Tommy put on as contrite a face as he could conjure. "I know that I've been mean to you. I would like to forget all that and be friends. Can't you forgive me?" *She's so stupid and easy to trick,* thought the boy as he gloated over her confused state.

Watching the emotions playing across her face, Tommy thought, *if I give her too much time to think, she might wise up.* He coaxed, "We could be friends. Let's play a game together."

Hesitant, Angie asked, "What game?"

The spirits that whirled around the boy rejoiced and whispered in his mind, *You've got her now. Kill her! Kill her! She's not worthy of life. Kill her!*

Tommy tried not to gloat, but he knew he had her. "How about hmmm . . ." he paused as if he had to think of one. "How about Simon says?"

Angie remained silent, her face puzzled.

Tommy insisted, "Yeah, Simon says is fun. Come on, let's play. Soon I'll have to go home and we won't really be friends then, will we?"

Angie stared, and then a look of peace came over her. She laid her bike down and approached Tommy. Holding out her hand for a handshake, she announced, "We be friends now."

Tommy smiled and shook her hand. "Let's play. It's getting late. First, I'll be Simon, then you can be Simon."

"Okay," she answered

Tommy grinned. "Simon says: 'Stand facing me.'"

Positioning himself so his side was by the water, he made sure he stood closer to the edge of the lake that was protected by a large grove of pines.

Angie obeyed and laughed. "See, Angie know game."

Tommy waited until Angie faced him. She stood a few feet away from him, with her left side more toward the center of the icy lake.

"Now," Tommy hesitated as if he were thinking of the next move, "Now, 'Simon says: 'Take two giant steps to the left.'"

Angie hesitated. She had to start the sign of the cross to know what was left and what was right. "Two make me on lake."

"Me too," answered Tommy. "The lake is frozen. There's nothing to be afraid of."

Stupid down. She'll drown! She'll drown! snickered the Spirit of Murder as he danced around Tommy with delight.

Angie looked at the lake. "You be right. Lake all hard." She took two large side steps and now stood on the frozen surface.

Tommy also took two steps and stood facing her. "See, its fine. Now Simon says: 'Take five giant steps to the left.'"

Angie obeyed, realizing that Tommy was also taking the same steps. Out further on the lake now, Tommy watched as Angie looked around and her eyes became solemn.

"Maybe we go other way?" she asked quietly.

"Why, are you a chicken?" the brash boy teased.

"Angie no chicken," she answered.

"Then, Simon says: 'Take two giant steps back if you're not a chicken.'"

Looking around her, Angie paused.

"Angie's a chicken, Angie's a chicken," Tommy taunted.

Standing still, fear replaced her pensive look. "Me no want play. No more. Me need go home."

Tommy put on a disappointed face. It wasn't hard. He almost had her right where he wanted her. With a few more moves, she would be on the thin ice. He knew the ice would break and she was probably too stupid to know how to swim and save herself. He knew he would never save her. She would drown and he would be gone. Problem solved. No one would laugh at him again when she said her stupid poems. *Why would she want to live anyway? She was just a stupid down.*

Don't let her get away, whispered the Spirit of Rage in Tommy's ear. *Are you stupid? Are you going to let a dummy beat you?*

"I thought you wanted to be my friend. Why don't you want to play with me?" he asked.

"Me want play. Not on lake," she answered.

"Why don't you play fair? I'm Simon now. It's my turn. You'll get your turn soon."

"Me fair," Angie insisted. "Lake too icy."

"Aw, just a few more turns and you can be Simon, or are you a chicken?" he asked.

Angie had no poem for the name chicken. She wanted to be friends and not be a scare-dee cat. She followed his instructions and took two giant steps back. Nothing happened, even though the ice she now stood on was clear. Tommy grinned, he could see the water sloshing beneath the frosted surface. He also took two steps back, but his steps took him to the thicker ice, which had been protected by the shade.

"Now," the boy announced, "take four giant steps to the left."

"Ha, you no say Simon!" she answered.

Tommy laughed. "Okay, Simon says: 'Take four giant steps to the left.'"

Angie felt as if she was having fun now and soon it would be her turn to be Simon. She took four giant side steps that landed her in the center of the lake. Both children could hear cracking sounds coming from under her feet. Angie looked up in fear. Tommy tried to hide his elation as the water swirled wildly under the thin ice beneath her. A cold wind blew hard as the temperature of the warm, February day dropped with the sun.

Tommy took four giant steps to the left. He waited, sure the thin sheet beneath her would give out under her weight, but nothing happened. He could feel the cold sweat of horror as it ran down his back.

Angie turned and took a few steps toward the shore. "Me go home Now. Done with game."

Tommy panicked. He couldn't let her get away this time.

"Stop, don't go!" he shouted. Without thinking, the boy made a quick move to stop her. Running toward her, Tommy unwittingly brought his weight onto the thin ice. As the ice continued to crack, he grew elated. It's happening! She's going under! he thought gleefully. As the cracking sound grew louder, a look of terror crossed Angie's face.

Tommy gleefully announced, "See how stupid you are, you dumb down. Now you're going to drown."

Tommy dodged toward the left, trying to grab Angie before she could reach the thicker ice. Skidding on the slippery surface, he fell, hitting the ice hard. The cracking sound grew louder as the ice split apart. It only took an instant for Tommy to realize the breaking sound wasn't coming from under Angie's feet. Looking down, he saw the ice rapidly break beneath him.

There was no time to react and the ice he was on disintegrated. In the distance, he could hear Angie scream, but it was too late for him to recover. Tommy fell into the lake. The cold darkness swallowed him.

Fifteen

No one has greater love than this, to lay down one's life for one's friends.
(John 15:13)

Angie watched with horror as Tommy fell into the dark water. It was only a moment, but it seemed like an eternity. She watched his face reflect the growing realization of what was happening to him. She reached out, but was too far away to grab him. He disappeared beneath the darkness. Angie hesitated, wondering if she should go for help. As she took a step toward the shoreline, the ice crackled beneath her foot. She would never make it.

As she stood frozen with fear, it dawned on Angie that if she went for help, it would take too long. She would have to walk so slowly and carefully to get to the shore without falling into the water herself. And even if she did get to solid land safely, there was no one in the park to help her. Even if she rode her bike and found help, it would be too late. Tommy would be dead.

Looking at the open ice where he had fallen, Angie saw Tommy's hand reaching up grabbing frantically at the open air. She reversed direction and took a step toward him, the ice cracking loudly beneath her foot. Again she hesitated, not knowing what to do. *She couldn't leave him to drown, but how could she reach him?*

Angie heard a whisper, a lone thought within, "Play army."

What? she asked.

As if someone heard her thought, the voice answered, "Play

army."

Josh and Angie used to play a game years ago that imitated soldiers crawling along a battlefield. Josh was fascinated with war movies at the time and collected plastic soldiers. He would spend hours with his tiny warriors as they fought battle after battle on the desk in his room. When Moma thought he was isolating himself too much, she would order him to play outside. "You need fresh air," she would insist. Josh would object loudly. He hated to leave the battle on his desk unfinished. However, he obeyed.

Josh would drag Angie along, yelling, "Let's play army." He had a complete army outfit that included a toy rifle, a canteen, and a pair of binoculars. In the field behind their house, the one that ran along all the homes on their block, they would pretend to be attacking. Josh taught Angie to crawl on her elbows, pushing quietly with her feet, to drag along soldier style. They would use the binoculars to spy on all the neighbors. They spent spend hours in the field, planning one attack after another. Angie got quite good at hiding in the tall brush as she crawled soldierlike from house to house. Eventually, Josh grew out of his army phase. They hadn't played the game for years, but now Angie remembered.

Slowly, getting down on all fours, Angie laid on her stomach. She was terrified to make the first move, but she knew she didn't have much time. She crawled on her belly, slowly and carefully. Inch by inch, she made her way to the opening in the ice. She reached the hole just as Tommy's hand started to disappear beneath the water. Quickly reaching into the water, Angie grabbed his hand and gave it a powerful yank. Pulling hard with both hands, she brought his arm up until she had his shoulder out of the water.

Tommy's head quickly followed. He gasped for air and blubbered weakly, "Help me!"

With all the strength she could muster, Angie dug her fingers into the wet cloth of the boy's shirt, twisting the material to increase her grip. When she knew her hand was secure, hanging onto the shoulder of the boy's shirt, she made her move. Letting go with one hand, she grasped the other shoulder and yanked hard. With a firm grip on both the boy's shoulders, she slowly wiggled back across the ice until the edge of the hole cut under Tommy's ribs. It was as far as she could pull him.

The boy's thin body lay in an awkward position. His upper body was above water, lying on the ice, face forward. The rest of his body, from the ribs down, remained below. Angie was smaller and much lighter. No matter how hard she pulled, she didn't have the power to tug him completely out of the water. She concentrated on keeping her grip. It took all her might just to hold him.

"Help!" she screamed, only to hear her cries echo through the empty park. Her cries rang through the deserted park with only the birds and the squirrels to hear. She called for help until her throat grew sore and scratchy.

Tommy continued to mumble, "I'll kill her, I promise. Don't let Joe know."

She couldn't understand what he was talking about. "Don't talk. Me hold you."

Still, the boy mumbled without much sense. Angie didn't think Tommy could hear her. It seemed as if he was talking in his sleep.

Sometimes Josh would wake her up, talking in his sleep. He often had nightmares about monsters chasing him. At night he would call out for help, often yelling things that made little sense. Moma said it was from all the sci-fi movies Josh watched. When he yelled in his sleep, just as Tommy was doing now, he seemed in a world of his own. Tommy kept crying, "Mommy, Mommy! Come get me!"

His mother never answered and neither did Angie. She had screamed so hard for help that her throat ached. It took all her strength to hold onto the boy. She swallowed hard and used whatever voice she had left to call for help to what seemed like a deserted world.

Within a few minutes, her fingers grew numb and she was having trouble feeling the shirt she clutched. One shoulder came loose and, as the boy's arm slipped through her grip, she grabbed the wet shirt by the elbow. She couldn't feel her fingers and they didn't seem to be listening to her commands. Soon she only had him by his elbows. She pulled back, wiggling on the ice, hoping to keep him from slipping back into the water.

It worked for awhile and Angie shivered with the cold that now penetrated her clothing. She couldn't seem to stop shaking. Her mind drifted – she thought about all the people she had seen on her paper route. She wished she weren't so stupid. Maybe if she wasn't so slow, she could help them with their problems. She thought about Moma and wondered if she was worried yet.

She felt Tommy slipping away again. Angie couldn't feel her fingers at all now. She wiggled back as far as she could and found she was now holding him by his wrists. She used all her strength, but he was slowly slipping into the cold water. Angie found herself forgetting where she was. Her mind drifted from silly thoughts about the circus she had seen that summer to thoughts about school. She couldn't concentrate.

Tommy was so heavy and her hands and arms were so numb. She still held his hands in hers, but she was so tired. She just couldn't pull any more. Her legs were numb and seemed so useless. Angie brought her mind back to the situation. She was going to lose him. He had stopped talking. Raising her head up, she realized he had gone to sleep. He was dead weight now, not helping at all, and she could feel her grip weakening.

Angie panicked. She screamed for help, but no one answered. Her head hurt. *What me do?* Realizing there was only one thing to do, Angie scooted her body around and, sitting up, she held tight to Tommy's hands. Then letting go, she slipped into the water. The freezing cold shocked her, but she grabbed Tommy under his arms and pushed him forward onto the ice from behind. Angie kicked her feet to stay afloat.

Once again, Tommy was lying on the ice up to his waist as Angie held him from behind. She continued to call for help. She was so tired, her legs so heavy as if they weighed too much to move. The water seemed to thicken as she kicked. Angie knew that didn't make any sense, but many of her thoughts didn't make sense. As her mind continued to drift, she would forget where she was. Angie had to keep pulling herself back to the present and she put all her strength into pushing Tommy's limp body forward. It was a losing battle.

With each minute, she grew weaker and Tommy would slowly sink, inch by inch. Angie felt numb, but not afraid. Her emotions didn't make sense. She should be in a panic, yet she felt a strange calmness. She shook her head as her thoughts began to drift again.

"Help us, somebody – help us!" she shouted, without expecting to hear anyone answer.

"Hang on, I'm coming," a voice shouted.

At first, Angie thought she imagined the voice. Was someone there? Was someone coming?

"Help! Help!" she shouted, listening for the response.

"I'm coming!" the voice answered firmly. Angie could tell that the voice's owner was much closer now. What's more, she recognized Josh's voice.

Then Angie could see him, belly crawling toward them. He was just a few feet away when she spotted him.

"Josh, how you find?" she asked with sudden hope.

"Never mind. Just let me have him."

Grasping Tommy under the arms, Josh pulled the unconscious boy from the water. Dragging him slowly back toward the shore, Josh brought the boy over the thicker ice toward the heavily treed lake edge.

"Can you hang on till I get him to shore?" he shouted to Angie.

"Yeah," she answered. Angie felt so sleepy. She just wanted to go home. She tried to pull herself up on the ice, but had no strength. She kicked her feet slowly as she clung to the edge. She no longer felt cold and had stopped shivering a while back. In fact, she felt warm and sleepy. She watched Josh drag Tommy to safe ground. Her eyes were so heavy and, although she tried to keep them open, she couldn't seem to fight the need for sleep.

Maybe me close eyes just a minute, she mused. Angie closed her eyes and drifted off. She couldn't feel her hands anymore, not noticing she had let her grip loosen.

Josh dragged Tommy's body from the lake and onto firm ground. Pulling his cell phone out of his pocket, he dialed 911. Josh spoke quickly, "I'm out at the lake. Two children have fallen through the ice. I need help right away. It's an emergency!"

After a few questions the operator assured him that help was on the way. Josh looked down at Tommy. His skin was so blue, especially around the lips. Josh pulled off his jacket and covered the wet boy. Then he realized Tommy wasn't breathing. Josh remembered the CPR class he had taken last summer. He checked Tommy's neck and felt a weak pulse. Putting Tommy's head into the right position, Josh clamped the boy's nose shut and started mouth-to-mouth resuscitation.

He could hear the sirens as the paramedics approached the park. Josh was relieved. They could take over the emergency care while he got Angie out of the water. Josh continued mouth-to-mouth, and, just as the paramedics and police arrived, Tommy coughed and started breathing on his own.

The paramedics took over and Josh shouted to the police, "My sister! She's still out there."

Josh started to crawl out toward Angie when a tall policeman stopped him, "Let us go get her, son. We have all the safety equipment.

The officer clipped safety ropes to his lifejacket and pulled out a strange-looking rescue sled. Then he lay down and started out on the lake to where Josh pointed. Tommy, mumbling incoherently, was being loaded into an ambulance as another arrived for Angie. When one of the paramedics noticed Josh shivering, he draped the jacket around him.

Josh stood by the side of the lake waiting for Angie. He couldn't see her from where he was. He watched as the policeman stopped in the middle of the lake where the opening would be. He was shocked as he turned and came back empty-handed.

Josh couldn't wait. He started toward the opening. Two policemen stopped Josh, holding him as he struggled against their grip. The returning policeman tried to avoid looking at Josh and, when he reached the lake's edge, looked at his fellow officers and shook his head. Josh fought their grip and, breaking loose, made it halfway back to where Angie should have been, before they grabbed him again.

Josh could see the opening now. Angie wasn't there. He fell to his knees and screamed. Angie couldn't hear his scream, as her body floated beneath the ice.

Sixteen

He delivers me from mine enemies: yea, thou lifts me up above those that rise up against me: thou hast delivered me from the violent man.
(Psalm 18: 48)

Joe stiffened behind his newspaper as the doorbell rang. The bell seldom rang in this house. He had made sure that Shirley and the children were isolated, no friends or relatives bothered anymore. It hadn't been easy. Shirley was too friendly with the neighbors and it had taken him quite a while to clip her wings.

She hated loneliness and isolation and had fought him at first, insisting on her independence. One after one, Joe found fault with each neighbor, fighting over minor comments or imagined slights. Sometimes Shirley would argue, but in the end she always capitulated to Joe's will. Joe knew it wasn't that she believed him and all the imagined flaws of the neighbors. He knew it was the fear of losing him and her main source of income that had won the day.

Joe even managed to end the relationship she had with her sister. *That nosy bitch had been nothing but trouble from the beginning,* he remembered. It had taken a lot of work for him to convince Shirley her sister was jealous. Shirley had been close to her sister all her life. They had shared a room while children, and all the games and imagined fantasies children create. Her sister had helped her financially when her husband deserted her. Shirley loved her sister with all her heart and had no intention of leaving such an important part of her life behind.

Joe worked at his plan slowly and carefully. Planting seeds of doubt in Shirley's mind with off-handed comments and innuendoes that nipped at his wife's insecurities, he watched as her faith in her sister's love began to crumble. That's when he made his move. The final straw that broke the friendship was convincing his wife that her sister had attempted to seduce him. Shirley clung to her need. She had always needed a man to take care of her and she dumped her sister quickly.

That bitch of a sister was hard to convince, thought Joe. When Shirley didn't answer phone calls, her sister came sniffing around the house. It took a restraining order to keep her away and persuade her that Shirley didn't want her around.

If the doorbell was ringing, it had to be because Tommy had gotten in trouble. Joe didn't want attention drawn to his family, but that damn kid just kept attracting the interest of outsiders. The first time, just a few months ago, it had been the school, investigating the reason Tommy got in so many fights. *Well, at least the fights had explained the numerous bruises on the kid's body,* Joe gloated.

However, he hadn't liked the look in Tommy's teacher's eyes. *That bitch thought she was so smart. I'd like to beat some sense into her,* he thought as he remembered the way she acted. She looked unconvinced, suspicious. She regarded Joe with that snotty look he hated. *People with educations always thought they were smarter, better than him.* Joe had outsmarted her and proved her wrong. Without concrete proof, she had to settle for Joe's explanation.

The second time, it had been the damn police, who had caught Tommy shoplifting downtown. Joe was able to handle that one with a "boys will be boys" attitude, promising a swift punishment He couldn't imagine what that brat had been up to all day. He steeled himself, and rose to answer the door. Looking through the front-door glass, Joe could see two policemen standing on the porch. Joe ordered Shirley and the twins back to the kitchen. He would have to take control of this situation. *Heaven only knows what stupid thing Shirley would say,* thought the dark man. *Well, I didn't marry her for her brains.*

When the girls were safely in the kitchen, Joe unlocked the door. He was afraid and he didn't like to be afraid. *Someone would have to pay for this.*

"Hello, sir," announced the younger officer. "Is this the home of Tommy Ellis?"

Damn! I knew it was that brat, he thought.

"Yes, may I help you?" Joe answered.

"Are you Tommy's father?" asked the officer.

"No, I'm his stepfather. What's this all about?" Joe was starting to get worried.

"Is the boy's mother available?" the officer remained resolute.

Joe stepped out on the porch, partially closing the door behind him, "

"His mother is inside. Is something wrong? She's a very nervous type." Joe stood blocking the door.

The two officers looked at each and capitulated to Joe's request.

"I'm afraid there's been a tragic accident," started the taller officer. "Your stepson was involved in a drowning, where he and another child fell through the ice on the lake. The little girl didn't survive and Tommy is in critical condition over at the hospital. We can drive you and your wife over to the hospital if you wish."

As terror overcame him, the blood drained from Joe's face. "No, I'll take his mother over to the hospital. Let me tell her. She'll panic if the police tell her."

"Fine, sir, and rest assured the police department is launching a complete investigation into the matter," announced the officers as they departed for their car.

Joe watched from the porch as the cops walked toward their squad car. As one turned to the other, Joe could hear them talking.

"That's really something. That stepfather really cares about that boy. He almost fainted when we told him. My stepfather never gave a damn about me."

If Joe hadn't been so worried about the situation, he would have laughed. He closed the door and leaned back against it. He took a moment to think and steady his trembling hands. *Why was this happening to him?* He tried so hard, so hard. Even as a child, Joe could not control the fits of rage that plunged him into playground beatings and constant trouble. *It's not my fault,* he thought. People never knew enough to shut up. They just keep pushing him.

According to his family and the school, it was always Joe's fault. They all blamed him, even when his sister made that nasty remark. She just keep pushing and pushing until he had no choice. He beat her so hard that she had to be hospitalized. Still, the family had learned to protect Joe and blamed the injuries on an unknown assailant outside the home. Later that evening, after his family had returned from the hospital, Joe's father confronted him about his behavior.

"I want you to get the hell out of this house," his father shouted. Joe wanted to kill him. It took all his strength to resist the urge to punch the old man. Fear kept his fists clenched at his sides, the fear that his father would call the police with the truth about his sister. Joe packed a knapsack and left, carrying his anger with him. Alone, on his own, he reasoned things might change.

Things had changed. As Joe grew into a man, the fits of anger also grew. When the red pain of rage descended on him, there was no outlet. The only thing that relieved the pressure was to strike out and the only way to let go of the pain was to give it to someone else. Joe had left a trail of victims in his wake as he moved from town to town and job to job. Sometimes he just barely escaped the police and the questions that would surely be followed by a charge of assault. Seven years ago, he had found Shirley. He prayed that marriage and a family would help.

Now what am I going to do? Joe worried as he rubbed his face with both hands. When they examined Tommy they would know. They would know that Joe was the one who caused the injuries. They would come and get him – take him away from his family and everything he loved. There was no way he could talk his way out of it this time. There was only one thing to do.

Within a minute he took action, shouting, "Shirley, girls – get upstairs and start packing. We've got to go. You've got five minutes – just five minutes so just take clothes for a week and anything you want to keep!"

Joe frantically dragged the luggage out of the hall closet as the women of the house entered the hall in complete confusion.

"What are you talking about? Where are we going?" questioned Shirley. His silence was her only answer.

"Daddy, we were going to the library," announced the twins in unison.

After he had gathered the suitcases, Joe growled, "Don't give me any lip. Just get upstairs and pack as quickly as you can. Don't take too much – just one suitcase each. Shirley, pack my clothes and shaver. Just empty the drawers and the medicine cabinet. Now go. You have only five minutes to pack and get in the car."

As the girls scrambled up the stairs, Joe went to his desk. He always kept the desk drawers locked. Taking his keys from his pocket, he unlocked the bottom drawer, and pulled out a small safe. Using another key to open the safe, Joe removed all the packets of money, and pushed them deep into his jeans pocket. *Where will I go?* He started to panic. *It doesn't matter, I've got to get out of here and I've got to do it quickly.*

While Joe waited impatiently, Shirley helped the girls pack. They were crying too hard to do a good job. She sent them down to their father and began to fill a quick bag for herself and Joe. Pulling things from the chest of drawers and the closet, she pushed in as much as she could before closing the zipper. Running to Tommy's room she grabbed a knapsack and stuffed in his underwear and shirts.

Joe appeared at the door, "Come on, Shirley, what's taking so long?" Then he saw the knapsack. "We won't need any of Tommy's things, so come on now. The girls are waiting in the car," Joe announced as he grabbed Shirley's arm and steered her toward the hall. Picking up the suitcases, he drew her toward the stairs.

Shirley pulled back. "What do you mean we won't need Tommy's things? Where's Tommy? We can't leave without him."

Joe's face reddened with anger. "Don't be silly. I'll explain everything when we get in the car. Now move it. We've no time to waste."

Shirley hesitated. "We're going to pick him up somewhere? That's what you mean, isn't it?"

Joe just nodded. He needed to get on the road. There was no time. The police could be on their way already.

Securing everyone and their things in the car, Joe took a look at the house that had been his home for the last seven years. He loved this house. It was so much better than the tiny home he grew up in. He had always dreamed of having a home like this and had been proud to raise his family here. Joe didn't like to think of the man who had actually purchased this home and paid off the mortgage. He hated to leave what he considered to be his. *I don't have a choice – they'll take it all away now because of that damn boy.*

Pulling out of the drive, he tried to think of where he should go. He decided to drive out of town, past the hospital. That way if anyone was watching, it would look as if they were going to see Tommy. It might buy them some time.

"Where are we picking up Tommy?" asked Shirley nervously.

"Don't worry about it. Let me concentrate on my driving," answered Joe without looking at her. Shirley was quiet, a little too quiet for Joe. He knew her well enough to feel the wheels turning in her mind. He had to think straight and she was just a distraction. *Why couldn't she just listen? What did she expect?* It was her son that had caused the problem.

She persisted, "Why don't you answer me? Where's Tommy?"

Joe was getting annoyed. He knew her. She would just keep it up until he answered her. They would never get Tommy. In fact, Tommy was the reason they had to leave their home. If it wasn't for that stupid kid, everything would be fine. Tommy was as stupid as his mother.

I can't listen to this nonsense. I have to shut her up, thought Joe.

He didn't give it much thought. It just came out. "Tommy's

dead," Joe answered. "I didn't want to tell you until we were settled. He fell through the ice in the lake and drowned."

Shirley didn't shut up. She screamed, "My baby! My baby! We have to go and bury my baby!" When the screams stopped, she wept.

"Don't be stupid, Shirley. They'll do an autopsy. They'll know he had a beating just this morning. They don't know what a handful he was. They'll arrest me. Is that what you want?" Joe asked with agitation.

Shirley was lost in her grief and continued to weep and scream for her baby. It was more than he could stand. She was the whiniest woman he had ever known. He couldn't stand listening to her and he couldn't think straight with her bawling. Now to top it - the girls are crying in the backseat. Joe cringed. Color rose in his cheeks as his anger grew.

"It's your fault! My baby is dead because of you!" she shouted.

Joe's silence was eerie. He just continued driving. They were halfway through the town and Joe seemed calm. Without a word, he continued down the Main Street, past the storefronts and onto the street lined with well-maintained Victorian houses. They would soon be passing the very lake that caused the accident.

"Stop! Just stop driving! Take me to the hospital. I want to see my baby," screamed Shirley.

Joe continued to drive in total silence. Shirley was distraught. She tossed and turned in her seat, unable to contain her emotions. Her facial expressions vacillated between pain and anger as each fought for dominance. She rattled the handle of the locked door in a futile attempt to escape the car.

"Let me out!" she shrieked, "I'll walk to the morgue. I won't tell anyone where you are. Let me out!"

Joe's silence continued and she couldn't sit still. Snapping off her seatbelt, she turned toward Joe and screeched, "If you don't let me out or take me to see Tommy, then the first chance I get, I'll call the police and tell them just where to find you."

Each time she yelled, the girls cried harder. Joe could feel the rage beginning.

He drove past the hospital with his eyes darting, watching for police cars that might be searching for him. He didn't care that inside the hospital, on the third floor, Tommy was unaware of his family rushing by. Deep in a coma, with machines beeping around him, Tommy slept. The nurses that changed his intravenous fluids wondered what would become of the child. Many didn't think he would live. Most prayed he wouldn't, believing he would be a vegetable if he did.

Seeing the hospital, Shirley screamed, "Is my baby in there? Is Tommy's body in there?"

Before Shirley could say another word, Joe reached across the seat and slapped her face so hard that her head bounced off the side window. The shock silenced both her and the girls.

Reaching up, Shirley touched her dripping lip. Holding her red-stained fingers in front of her, she stared at the blood as if she didn't know what it was. With her eyes opened wide, she turned and stared blankly at the hospital they were now passing. She had wondered what she would do without her son. Now she knew. Shirley finally understood her new role in the family.

She would take Tommy's place.

Seventeen

Blessed are you when they insult you and persecute you and utter every kind of evil against you (falsely) because of me. Rejoice and be glad, for your reward will be great in heaven. (Matt 5:11)

When Josh pulled the unconscious Tommy from the water, Angie experienced a sense of lightness, a feeling of being free. Angie had been sinking and so tired. She felt as if she had been carrying Tommy's weight for such a long time and now that heavy burden had been lifted. She forced her weary legs to kick to keep above water, struggling against profound fatigue. Now that the weight of Tommy's life was removed, Angie's eyes burned with weariness. She wanted to close them for just a moment. Her hands were cramped with pain from clinging to the heavy boy.

She flexed her numb fingers as they held the edge of the ice, just for a moment, but in that moment she lost her grip. She felt herself slipping into sleep. Angie didn't have the strength to fight. She slipped into a state of unawareness, until she felt Josh's strong arms lift her up, up from the frozen water.

His arms felt so warm and safe. Angie's apathy left her. When she opened her eyes, she expected to see her brother and instead she saw a most beautiful angel. His hair was like spun gold and it flowed freely in the wind as he carried her high above the lake. His eyes were a golden hazel. They flashed with a twinkling light that caught the sun's radiance, reflecting it like mirrors. A loose gown of shining silk twisted in the wind as he held his charge with gentleness. Angie was amazed.

"Who are you?" she asked.

He smiled. "I'm your angel. I've been with you since you were conceived."

"Why didn't I ever see you?" asked the girl

"You didn't need to, but I have always been there. And I will be with you for eternity," he answered softly.

"Where are we?" Angie paused and reached up to touch her lip. She couldn't feel the scar from her cleft palate operation. Her eyes opened wide with shock.

"Why am I speaking so well?" she whispered cautiously.

Her angel whispered, "Because you are coming into your reward. You used your limited vocabulary to teach the truth of God. Now you will speak with more clarity and with a purer voice than anyone in heaven."

"I don't understand," Angie exclaimed.

The angel laughed. "You will. You will have a higher understanding and knowledge than most in heaven. You see, Angie, Our Lord is a God of justice. You did not let your disability make you bitter and angry. Instead you overcame the barriers in your life to give love and kindness. In heaven, those who were blind may see colors that no one else can see. Those who were lame run the fastest. Those who were deaf hear notes of music no one else can enjoy. You will be especially smart and articulate. On earth your prayers were so powerful because of the suffering you offered up. Now you will be rewarded."

"Is that where I am going – heaven?" Angie whispered.

"Yes," the angel continued, "but don't be afraid. There is someone there who has been waiting to see you. She has been praying for you since you were born."

Angie's eyes opened wide with delight. "My mother! Will I see her?"

The angel smiled and nodded. "She has been waiting for you."

Angie paused for a moment as she seemed to remember

something important. "What about Moma and Josh? Is Tommy alright?"

"Don't worry about Moma. She will be coming soon. Josh has his whole life to live. You can watch over him and pray for him. Tommy really needs your prayers. He is in real trouble. Will you pray for him?" her angel asked.

Angie didn't respond. She seemed deep in thought for a moment. Her mind was so clear, her intellect so lucid. She had never experienced thoughts that came so easily, swiftly flowing through her mind. It was as if a dark cloud had been lifted and, with its disappearance, a light shone. The light revealed knowledge; knowledge that now seemed so simple, so easy to see. Her understanding was now so deep. Why hadn't she understood all these things before this supernatural moment?

"Would my prayers in heaven be more powerful if I just remained as I was on earth? In other words, without my reward?" she asked.

"Yes. Prayers are always more powerful with sacrifice. Is that what you wish?" asked the angel.

"Me be Angie. Me be me," announced the smiling child.

The angel glowed brighter with pride, "Yes, and Jesus will be so pleased to meet the Angie he created."

Maria trembled as she called the paper. It wasn't hard to reach the person she needed, only three people worked at the local tabloid. She asked about the photo and was almost instantly put on the line with the photographer.

"Where was the picture taken that was printed on the second page? Yes, the one with the illegal immigrants who live in the woods."

Maria's heart pounded as she waited for the answer.

The photographer had a long drawl. "Yes, ma'am, I know the one you're referring to. It's in the wooded area right behind the high school, just 300 yards into the woods. But I wouldn't go out there alone, ma'am, it could be dangerous."

"Don't worry – I won't be alone." Maria hung up quickly.

Calling the children, she was dismayed at how dirty their play had made them, "Quick, get washed up and dressed. Boys help your sister."

Maria scurried to her bedroom and, changing into warmer clothing, stood before the mirror brushing her long, dark hair. *I wonder what he will think of me. He hasn't seen me in almost three years. Suppose he doesn't want me?* Always, in the back of her mind she had carried that fear. *Suppose he had disappeared on purpose. Suppose he had found someone else.* Maria had no basis for the fears she experienced. She realized it was just her own insecurities that keep surfacing.

Now is no time to think about these things. I have my miracle, she thought. However, as she gathered the children, she still wondered what she would discover when she talked to Manuel. She decided not to tell the boys about her discovery.

As they waited at the bus stop, two ambulances sped by headed for the park. Maria blessed herself and finished her prayer for whoever needed the ambulances just as the bus arrived. It was a short ride to the high school and the bus let them out on the corner. As she walked down the drive to the back of the school, the children balked. They wanted to know why they were there and where they were going. Maria remained silent. *How can I say when I don't even know where I am going or where this discovery will lead me,* she thought.

The sun was low in the sky and Maria wanted to be out of the woods before dark. She quickened her pace as she carried her daughter in her arms. The woods were carpeted with dry, brown leaves left over from autumn. It was so silent with the birds gone south for the winter. Only the footsteps of her sons echoed through the grove.

Within ten minutes, Maria could hear the voices of the men as they carried from the camp. *What if Manuel was no longer there to protect them? Was she leading her children into danger?* pondered Maria. She had no choice. She had come so far to find Manuel. *How could she turn in fear now?* She prayed for protection as they reached the area in the woods that was the camp.

A circle of tents surrounded a large opening that contained a huge fire. Men sat around the fire laughing and joking in Spanish. They didn't notice Maria and the children until she stepped forward. The entire camp fell silent at the appearance of a stranger and three children. Some of the men rose and came toward Maria, who now stood frozen with fear. A man appeared from a tent and his call stilled the approaching men.

"Maria, is that you?" the weak voice called.

Turning her gaze in his direction, she answered, "Manuel, it is me and your children."

No words were spoken as he ran to her, holding out his arms. She folded into his embrace and right back into his love. The fear left, as she held him, noting the thin frame beneath the flannel shirt. Suddenly, the men in camp erupted in cheers as Roberto and Juan realized what was happening and started to cry. The two boys joined the hug that their parents shared and wept.

Finally, pulling back, Manuel stared at Maria with tearful eyes, "And who is this?" he asked as he smiled at the little girl.

"This is your daughter, Anna," answered Maria.

Manuel tried to hold the girl but she clung to her mother. "Ah . . . she doesn't know me," Manuel stated.

"But she will," answered Maria. "We've come to take you home."

Manuel gathered up his small knapsack of possessions as the other men in the camp slapped him on the back and congratulated him.

Walking with her now-completed family out of the woods to the bus stop, Maria had many questions. This, she knew, was not the time to ask them. The boys talked nonstop to their father. They had missed him so much. She was glad of the distraction. Her emotions fluctuated between joy and fear. *Why had he stopped writing? And why did he live in such a place?* She would wait until they were home in the little, yellow ranch, to indulge her curiosity. *First, I will feed the man. He is so thin.*

On their walk home from the bus stop, Maria stopped to purchase some food from the bodega with part of the $100 she had received in the mail. When Manuel saw the little ranch, he wept. Maria wondered how hard his life had been and what had brought him to living in a tent in the woods. She cooked his favorite food, enchiladas, as he sat with the children who clamored for his attention. Sitting around the kitchen table as a family filled Maria's heart with such joy that she couldn't stop smiling. She watched as Manuel ate more than two portions before he was satisfied. *What has he been through?* she wondered.

It was like a dream, him being here with the children. She had searched for him for so long, it was hard to accept that her search was over. *But was it?* She still had to find the reason for his disappearance. *What if there was another woman? What if he no longer wanted her,* she worried.

The uncertainty was too much. She had to find out. Maria started the dishes and ordered the children into their bedclothes. She had to be alone with Manuel. Drying the last dish, she finally found herself alone with her husband. Frightened as she was, she had to ask the question.

"Manuel, why were you gone so long? Why did you stop writing?" she whispered softly, afraid of the answer.

"I am so ashamed." He hung his head. "I am ashamed to tell you."

With fear gripping her heart, she sat beside him. "Don't be afraid. You should never be afraid of the truth. Tell me the truth, Manuel."

"I have been in prison, Maria," he blurted out. "I was too ashamed to let you know."

Maria's eyes opened wide and she gasped before answering. "In prison? For what?"

"When I first came over, I found a good job, a job in a pizzeria. The owner was an Italian immigrant and he taught me how to cook the pies. I was working six days a week, twelve hours a day. I looked forward to sending the money home and having you and the children join me. The owner had a nephew who he brought over from Italy. He arrived just two weeks after I started.

That's when the trouble began – money started missing. One night, just twenty days after I began working, the police arrived. The owner directed them to the back and they searched my things. To my surprise, they found hundreds of dollars tucked inside the lining of my coat."

Manuel wiped a tear away. "I was shocked. The police arrested me, while the owner and the nephew watched as they took me away. I had to sit in prison, waiting for a trial. I had no money for bail." Again Manuel stopped, trying to compose himself.

"Manuel, I'm so sorry." Maria reached out and held the broken man in her arms.

Silent for a few minutes, Manuel then continued. "I had no proof that I didn't steal the money. I couldn't understand how the money had found its way into my jacket. Sitting in jail I began to suspect that it was all a setup. The real thief had to find a way to divert attention from his own guilt. The judge gave me two years. While in prison I heard that the owner discovered that his nephew was stealing his money. He banned his nephew from his home and his business, but never did anything to exonerate me. I did my full sentence and just got out of prison a few months ago. I actually considered myself lucky because I was never deported."

Gazing at his wife, Manuel choked up. "I'm so sorry Maria. I was too ashamed to contact you. I wanted to find a job and get back on my feet. I was so humiliated."

"Shh. . . it's over now. I have a good job. You will find one. Once we save enough, we'll go home," Maria announced firmly.

The children came back in their nightclothes and surrounded their father. His joy was evident. He wept quietly as he hugged each child in turn.

For the first time in years, Maria felt a sense of peace. Her family was whole once more. She would never let them be separated again.

Silently she praised Mary. *Lady of Guadalupe – you have kept your promise. I have found my husband and I thank you for your intercession.* The peace was broken by the phone ringing. Maria was sure that no news could destroy her joy.

Answering the phone, Maria was surprised to hear Mrs. Larsen. "Hello, Maria. I know you weren't supposed to start until tomorrow morning, but I need you here tonight."

Maria was stunned, "I don't understand. . ." Her voice trailed off in confusion.

"There's a town meeting and I'm going. I need you to go with me. I will pay you a bonus, but you need to get over here right away." Mrs. Larsen's voice was agitated and quick.

Maria spoke without thinking, "Go out? You never go out!" Reaching up to cover her mouth, she realized what she had said.

There was a pause on the phone and then, without anger, the woman on the line answered, "That's true, but some things are more important than the past. Come immediately!" Maria heard the phone click before she could respond. Looking at her family, Maria knew that leaving was the last thing she wanted to do. She wanted to call the woman back. She didn't want to let her newly found husband out of her sight, but knew she didn't have a choice.

As much as she hated to think it, finding Manuel just meant she had another mouth to feed. That was until he found a job and could help. Maria was behind in everything. She only had what was left of the $100 that had been found in the mailbox. *No, I will have to go. If I don't, I might lose this job*, she resolved. *She needed the job. They needed the money.*

Eighteen

And they said one to another, we are verily guilty concerning our brother, in that we saw the anguish of his soul, when he besought us, and we would not hear; therefore is this distress come upon us. (Gen. 42:21)

The wrongs we have committed during our youth often rise from our memories to accuse us. Yet, we forget the sins of omission. These are not like regular sins. They are the things that we should have done or could have done, but didn't. For example, that dollar you meant to give to the homeless man on the corner. You never did it because you were afraid he would expect a dollar every morning. Or how about that phone call to a needy friend – you reached for the phone but stopped. She would just bring you down with all of her problems. How about that shy child who stood in the corner of the playground? You meant to talk to her – to build up her confidence. However, your friends were playing a game you couldn't miss and so that conversation never happened. We often think that sins of omission couldn't be as important as actual sins. It's a funny thing, but when we are older and humbled by life, it is the things we didn't do which we regret the most.

Maria walked the two blocks from the bus stop. She was shocked to see Mrs. Larsen standing on the front porch with a coat and hat on, clinging to a handbag. The redhead stood with her back rigid and her head held high, staring stiffly ahead.

Looking around, she spotted Maria headed her way, and her tight, facial expression relaxed. "Maria, come, take my arm, we're going to town hall. You guide me. I have to look straight ahead – not at the stares of my nosy neighbors."

Maria took the tall woman's arm and, with the resolve of a General going into battle, Mrs. Larsen marched down the steps, out of the gate, and onto the sidewalk. They continued on toward the municipal building that was in the center of town. Numerous people did stop and stare, some with their mouths open. Mrs. Larsen marched on, clinging to Maria's arm for support.

As they approached the town hall, they saw a large crowd standing outside. Apparently, those present were waiting for the front door to open and they droned on in angry whispers. Occasionally a voice would rise, giving accentuated emotion to the pain the crowd was feeling.

As Mrs. Larsen and Maria approached, a stunned silence fell upon the gathering. Walking with her head held high, Mrs. Larsen momentarily hesitated as everyone stared. Maria pressed her arm, encouraging her forward. With a deep breath, she continued, her pause unnoticed by others. In silence, the crowd parted as she approached the door of town hall.

The building, with ornate carvings and massive columns was graced by a substantial double door. It stood as testimony to the pride of the last century. As Mrs. Larsen reached the doors, a loud clicking of the locks announced the opening of the hall. It was as if the inhabitants had been awaiting the arrival of the queen to allow entrance. The redhead and her darker companion were the first to enter the hall, followed by the seemingly lesser townies.

Harold, with his eyes red from crying, held the door open for the crowd to enter. Tien Ca'Le and Mrs. Lennon sat right behind the two women. Ruthie, still wearing her waitress uniform and dragging her four children, found her seat across the aisle. Reverend Huber, arriving late from his church, scanned the room for a seat. He

spotted one in the front and found himself sitting next to Tien Ca'
Le. Harold was shocked to see Moma and Josh slip quietly into the
rear row of the hall. Moma settled back in her seat, eyes swollen from
weeping. Josh's face was tight and red. He looked angry.

Angie's death has to be someone's fault, Josh's mind screamed. He
had to find someone besides himself to blame. Although logically
it was not his fault, in his heart he did blame himself. His heart
whispered questions. *Why did I pull Tommy to shore first? Why did I
leave Angie waiting in the water?* Over and over the painful questions
would rise. Josh pushed them down. They were too much to bear.
Somehow he knew that if he allowed himself to look at the questions,
he would drown in his grief.

Josh didn't have a choice. He had to come to the meeting because
he wanted to know – no, he really needed to know the latest findings
related to Angie's accident. Perhaps there would be an answer here,
something that would soothe the pain burning in his soul. Moma
couldn't let him go alone. Now that she had lost Angie, she couldn't
bear to have Josh out of her sight. People in the back were shocked to
see them. Little was said, however, as the meeting was starting. Since
all were anxious to hear what the mayor had to say, only minute
words of sympathy were exchanged.

Harold leaned against the back wall. The wainscoted hall with
its elaborate carvings had never hosted so large a crowd. At the
podium stood the rotund Mayor, stunned by the procession of people
who quickly filled the rows of chairs, while the spillover lined the
walls. On an upper deck sat the council chamber with a long desk
and microphones between them and the murmuring mob.

"Hm-hum," the mayor cleared his throat repeatedly until the
crowd settled down.

"I call this town meeting to order," began the mayor, "and I request a reading of the minutes of the last meeting."

An older man stood up. The man Angie always called "old-crab-face" spoke loudly. "We're not here to listen to a bunch of bureaucratic hob-gobbin. We want to know about the lake!"

The mayor's face reddened as the crowd grew louder in its displeasure. "Now, now," he cautioned with a false smile, "We will dispense with the readings of the minutes and get to the main concern of our fellow citizens."

"Well, get on with it then!" yelled a voice from the back of the room. "What are you going to do about the lake and what happened to those children?"

"Well, it certainly was a tragic accident. We are so sorry that it happened," answered the mayor as he used a large handkerchief to wipe the perspiration off his round face. "However, as you know, the township had a sign posted. The sign clearly forbids anyone to walk upon the icy lake. The sign relieves the township of any liability in this matter."

Harold could feel the anger rising inside him. The mayor only cared about the bottom line, not Angie. The crowd rumbled with discontent at his remark and the quick-thinking politician made his way out of the limelight. "The Chief of Police is here to give us the latest developments in this tragic case."

The mayor, who was usually happy to be the center of attention, was glad to give the podium to the elderly, soft-spoken Chief. The crowd quieted, anxious to hear the well-loved policeman's findings.

"Mr. Mayor, fellow citizens, we held a shift strategy meeting late this afternoon and have decided that in the future we will post an officer to patrol the park. A sign is usually not enough to prevent a child from taking a horrible risk or to stop a crime from happening. I feel that an officer close enough to help might have prevented the tragedy which occurred today. I am sorry to announce we recovered Angie's body just before sundown today." The Chief bowed his head and paused, as the crowd moaned with pain.

Harold felt as if he had been punched in his stomach. *My little friend, so cold and alone under the ice,* he thought. He took a deep breath to still the sobs that fought to escape from his burdened heart. His knees felt weak with the emotional blow and the finality of the police recovering her diminutive body. Harold felt faint as he leaned against the wall. I have to find a place to sit, he thought as he walked slowly up the center aisle. Spotting a seat on the right, he was surprised that it wasn't taken.

The four children by the seat were restless and squirmy. Most of the people wanted to avoid the distraction of sitting next to them. Harold took advantage of the situation to sit and regain his strength. He couldn't stand the thought of what had happened to Angie, but he couldn't stand the thought of not knowing the whole truth either. As he sat, he trying to quiet his heart, Harold turned and, looking at the children, noticed their mother for the first time. She was an attractive woman in her forties, wearing too much makeup and a too-tight waitress uniform.

As Harold looked, a memory came. He started to smile. Now I know, he mused, my little friend isn't gone at all. She is watching over me. The pain left his heart as a supernatural sense of Angie's presence overpowered him. He had to smile.

Reaching over, he extended his hand to the woman. "Hello, is your name Ruthie?"

Taken aback, the woman smiled. "Why, yes, how did you know?"

"Angie – Angie told me so much about you. She loved you so. I feel as if I know you."

Ruthie blushed with pleasure, "I loved Angie. It's nice to know she thought of me as a friend."

Harold turned as the speaker at the podium continued. Ruthie looked down. Harold's feet were firmly planted on the ground.

The Police Chief continued with the findings, "Preliminary studies indicate that the cause of death was drowning facilitated by hypothermia. Of course, we'll know more after the autopsy. There is no doubt that Angie's death was a tragic accident. However, an investigation must be made. As for the other child, his name is

Tommy Ellis. He's in intensive care and is still comatose. We will all pray for his recovery. We're still investigating why the two children were playing on the lake."

Before he could continue, a voice from the side of the hall shouted, "They weren't playing. My sister is a nurse at the hospital. That boy may be unconscious, but he's talking. He's rattling on and on about how he's going to trick Angie. Laughing about how he's going to kill her by luring her out on the thin ice. I always knew that kid was no good. I think he was stealing from the bakery."

The crowd's shocked murmurs filled the hall as anger rose quickly. A male voice sounded above the fray, "I knew that kid was no good! I had to kick him out of my store every week. I think he was stealing fishing lures, but I could never catch him. I'm not surprised he killed that girl!"

It took the Police Chief a few minutes to calm the crowd, "We have some new information on the boy. I've been informed that he has unmistakable signs – signs confirming years of physical abuse. The evidence of extensive abuse are fractures both treated and untreated, permanent lacerations of the liver, with fresh and widespread bruises and lacerations in various stages of healing. It seems Tommy has been brutally and continuously beaten for many years. The child must have lived in constant pain and fear of his abuser. Yet no one seemed to notice. Except for a minor investigation precipitated by a teacher, no one in our town seemed to be aware of the terrible situation in which that boy lived."

The crowd was silenced by the stunning news; however the silence only lasted a moment as the focus of anger shifted.

Reverend Huber, awakened from his grief, had the memories of his own old wounds re-opened. The pain of those memories rose up from his spirit as the list of the boy's injuries was announced. Jumping to his feet, he asked loudly, above the crowd's droning, "Who abused the child?"

The Chief was glad to refocus the anger. "We have reason to believe he was beaten by his stepfather. An investigation into the man's record revealed a history of angry outbursts that resulted in numerous episodes of assaults and fights. Although he was never convicted, clearly he was headed in that direction."

"Did you arrest the man?" a voice shouted from the crowd.

The crowds' angry murmurs grew. Now they had someone new on which to vent their rage. It saved them from thinking of their own responsibility in the matter. As the rumbling quickly became louder, the Chief realized the crowd was in danger of becoming a mob. Fearing their anger and vigilante spirit would lead to violence, he sought to calm the multitude before him.

The Chief shook his head and appeared disturbed to relate what had happened next. "Once we were made aware of the circumstances, we went to the Ellis home to facilitate an investigation and a probable arrest. What we found was that the suspect and the entire family had escaped. We pursued, but they must have gotten a good head start. They may even be out of the state by now. Of course, we have put out an APB, but depending on the man's resources, it may be tough to pin them down."

For a moment the crowd grew silent, but with a new outlet for their anger, the outbursts began again. "Why didn't anyone notice the boy was abused?" demanded one man, while another asked, "Where were his teachers?"

"Sure, blame the teachers," answered one of the junior high school teachers. "Where were all the neighbors?!"

The Chief rubbed his head in exasperation as he tried without success to answer the rapid-fire questions that were being shouted. It seemed each question led to another and, with every unanswered question, the mood of the crowd became darker.

Finally, someone asked a question the Chief felt he could answer.

"What are they going to do with the boy now that his family has disappeared?"

The Chief jumped at a chance to calm the crowd. "The boy will have to be placed in a foster home, that is, once he recuperates. And we should all spend our time praying for Tommy Ellis's recovery."

The people in the room mumbled, until Mrs. Larsen stood up. As her voice rose in anger, the rest of the room fell silent. "I don't care where that boy is sent, but it better not be in this town. He killed Angie and we don't want him. In fact, we won't have him."

The Chief was so surprised that he began to stutter. "But. . . but, he's just a little boy and he's been so abused. Where do you think we would send him?"

Mrs. Larsen stood her ground. "I don't care where you send him. You can send him to hell for all I care. He'll not live in this town. We don't want him!"

The people in the hall took up the mantra and started to shout in unison, "We don't care. We don't want him."

Moma watched from the back. She was so distracted by her grief, her heart was so torn apart, that she found it hard to concentrate on what was being said. Detached, she watched as a thin, disheveled man entered the hall. In a threadbare, brown sweater he stood and listened to the crowd's emotional outbursts. Slowly he pushed ahead, walking up the aisle to the podium. Moma didn't recognize him until he walked up to the stage.

The crowd began ranting, their rage growing heated. They watched the man step up to the podium. The fellow asked the Chief if he could address the crowd and the Chief seemed relieved to relinquish his post. Gradually, the mob grew silent, curious about the man about to address them.

When the man took his place behind the podium and removed his hat to speak, Moma gasped. In the silent room, everyone gaped, looking first at Moma's stunned expression and then with renewed interest at the man who caused such a reaction. Despite the years and the physical changes, Moma would have recognized him anywhere as Artie, her son-in-law. The man who stood silently before the gathering was Josh and Angie's father.

In a soft voice, he started speaking. "I'm probably the last person, besides that boy, that Angie talked to this morning. I'm the last customer on her route."

"The coconut cake man," whispered Tien as she listened with interest.

Artie continued, "She came to see me every Saturday. She always brought me my favorite cake. We would sit and talk, sometimes for more than an hour. She was never in a hurry, I guess because I was her last stop. I didn't know who she was – just a handicapped girl who made my lonely life a little less bitter. I looked forward to her visit each week. This morning, we had a long conversation about forgiveness."

The crowd was hungry to hear about Angie and what her last moments were.

Artie said, "I told her why I was so alone. I told her that I had done something so terrible, so horrible that it was unforgivable. She said there was no such thing. Angie said if Jesus could forgive the men who crucified him, then there was no such thing as the unforgivable. I didn't understand her at the time and, worse, I didn't believe her."

Artie sobbed, and then took a deep breath, "Angie told me my problem wasn't that my family wouldn't forgive me. It was that I couldn't forgive myself. You see, that's why you're so angry. You think you're angry at that boy, Tommy, but you're really angry at yourselves."

For a moment the crowd remained silent, then the rumbling began again. The woman who worked in the bakery demanded, "Why should we forgive ourselves? We didn't kill Angie!"

"Ah, but we did. We all did," Artie insisted. "How long did that boy walk among us? How long was he hungry, neglected, and abused?" Looking directly at the bakery woman, Artie explained, "You looked at him and saw a thief – not a thin, hungry child."

The chubby saleswoman from the bakery sat down, hanging her head.

Artie continued, looking at the manager of the general store. "You looked at him and only saw his poverty, someone who couldn't add to your sales, not a lonely child with nowhere to go."

The store manager crossed his arms over his chest and looked away in irritation.

Artie sighed. "How many of us go around looking for someone to love us instead of looking for someone who needs love?"

Ruthie wiped the tear as it ran down her cheek.

The thin man at the podium hung his head as if in shame, "That boy wandered around our town, broken and abused. All of us, including myself, ignored him. We all locked ourselves away, lost in our own problems, ignoring the pain of those outside ourselves."

Mrs. Larsen gripped the arms of her seat.

Artie continued, "And because we ignored him, Angie died this afternoon. We are all responsible, but Angie wouldn't want us to wallow in our guilt. Angie was about forgiveness. I, of all people, should know about that. You see, long ago I betrayed Angie. I deserted her and didn't even know who she was when she came to me each Saturday. But she knew who I was."

Artie sobbed loudly. "I'm Angie's father."

Nineteen

May Christ dwell in your hearts through faith and may charity be the root and foundation of your life. (Eph. 3: 17)

The blood drained from Josh's face as the identity of the man behind the podium hit him. He looked at Moma for confirmation and she nodded. He stared at the man with a disbelief that soon turned to anger. Moma watched as his jaw clenched and his face hardened. All the pain Josh felt because of his sister's death was now fermenting into hatred toward the man who had deserted her.

Once the crowd's shock of this revelation wore off, Artie continued. "I was afraid. When my wife died, the thought of raising two children overwhelmed me. When the doctor told me that my baby girl had significant defects, I just ran. I ran away from my problems and my children. Just like this town is trying to run away from Tommy."

"Don't compare yourself to us!" an angry voice shouted.

"Oh, no," answered Artie. "What you're about to do is exactly what I did so many years ago. You're running away from your responsibility. We have ignored this boy for long enough and look what our apathy has done. Because we ignored his need, our Angie is gone." The man paused and sighed. "We have a second chance now. Let's not repeat our mistake. Let's all think of what Angie would do. Let's help this boy."

A deadly silence filled the room as each person examined his or her own thoughts and regrets in the matter.

Mrs. Larsen couldn't contain her rage. Jumping to her feet, she demanded, "Who are you to judge us? You deserted Angie. She was my little friend, my only friend. We don't want that boy. Every time we look at him, we'll remember what he did to Angie. You didn't care for her, but we loved her. I loved her. And we don't want that boy around!"

Artie bowed his head in humility and answered, "You're right. I have no desire to judge anyone. I don't have the right after what I did. That's not what I'm trying to do. I'm trying to save this town from making the same mistake that I did. Right now you think you can't forgive. You're ready to desert that boy. Believe me, when the pain is over, you'll be left with nothing but regret. Don't run away from the boy."

Mrs. Hansen looked annoyed. "I don't think I will ever regret keeping that boy from this town. No one wants him here. There is no home for him, foster or otherwise. I know I don't want him."

With great flamboyance, she turned to face the assembly. "Does anyone here plan to take him in? Will anyone in this town offer this murderer a home?"

The silence of the room supported Mrs. Hansen's premise. She turned back to the speaker and was about to make her point, when a lone voice echoed through the chamber. "I'll take him."

The shock left Mrs. Hansen speechless. It took her a few moments to compose herself. She turned to the room and demanded, "Who said that?"

She gasped when Moma rose. "I'll take him. Tommy can come and live with me."

Josh couldn't believe his ears. *What was Moma thinking?*

Moma gave Josh a look that silenced his question. Grabbing her coat and bag, Moma announced, "There, it's settled. Tommy will come and live in our house. Come now, Artie, it's time to go home."

Artie was sure he had misheard. However, Moma, now standing in the aisle, turned and repeated herself, "Artie, come. It's time to go home."

Stunned, Artie walked down the aisle as the crowd murmured. Taking his arm, Moma started toward the door. She suddenly stopped and turned to Josh who followed in shock.

"Josh," Moma said, "your father left his hat on the podium. Please go get it for him."

Josh reddened in anger and opened his mouth to speak. Another look from Moma stilled him. He was in the habit of obedience and turned to retrieve Artie's hat. Taking Artie's arm again, Moma led the man and the boy out the door as the crowd again became agitated.

"Well, I like that!" shouted the bakery saleswoman. "It's like Angie never lived."

The manager of the general store raised his voice above the buzz of the assembly. "She just thinks she's better than us. That's all!"

Harold rose and donned his coat. "It's not that she thinks she's better than us. It is simply that she is."

Turning to Ruthie, he asked, "May I escort you and your children home?"

Ruthie proudly took the arm he offered. Silently she said a prayer, a prayer of thanks to Angie.

Mrs. Hansen plopped into her seat. Her eyes wide open, stared straight ahead as she asked herself, *am I really so wrong? He killed my Angie, my friend.* Almost instantly she heard a voice from deep within her heart. *She's my Angie. And he's my Tommy. What do you think Angie would say about the whole situation?* She shook her head, refusing to listen.

Willing herself into her present surroundings, she heard Reverend Huber talking to the little Asian woman about abused children. Marie silently waited, hoping she would soon be home with her newly united family. The entire room was up and on their feet, donning their coats, as the mayor stood at the podium, droning on about the need to fix the potholes on Main Street. The meeting went on, but for the majority of the attendees, it was over. As the crowd fanned out their separate ways, the night swallowed them in darkness, leaving all to their lonely thoughts.

Josh watched Moma hold Artie's arm as they walked on the sidewalk toward home. They moved in silence; each holding his own thoughts. Josh followed behind, with his head hanging in sorrow and disbelief. *What just happened?* He wondered how things could change so quickly.

Josh's heart was broken, crushed by the guilt he felt for leaving Angie alone to drag that boy to safety. *Why didn't I pull her out of the water first? Why did I leave her alone?* He replayed the scene at the lake repeatedly, but couldn't see what he could have done differently.

Tommy was unconscious. If he had grabbed Angie first, Tommy would have slipped into the water and died. *Better him then Angie,* Josh thought. *If I couldn't save them both, I should have saved her!* It was useless to ponder it now. Josh knew that. At the lake he had thought Angie was strong enough to hold on. He thought he would be back in just a minute to save her. *Why did she let go?* His heart cried. *Why didn't she hang on for just a few minutes?*

Reaching the house ended Josh's speculations. He couldn't believe Moma was bringing that man to live in their home. It was bad enough Angie was gone – never mind that the father who deserted her seemed to be taking her place. Moma removed her coat and bustled around the kitchen preparing a late-night snack of reheated stew and bread. Artie, confused over what to do, removed his hat and sat at the kitchen table. This was more than Josh could bear. He went to his room, slamming the door in an attempt to close off the rest of the world, but his room was just off the kitchen and he could hear everything that was said.

Artie jumped at the sound. "Perhaps, I'd better go home."

Moma looked toward Josh's bedroom and answered, "This is your home. Here, have something to eat while I go and talk to him." She placed a bowl of stew before Artie and a plate of her crusty bread. Artie picked up his spoon.

"I can't stay tonight. I have George to care for."

"Who's George?" Moma asked.

For the first time she saw Artie smile. "George! Angie loved him."

Moma could see the love in his eyes as he thought of his daughter. "Then you'll go back tonight, but you and George will come home to stay tomorrow. Josh needs you, even if he doesn't know it yet. Finish your food while I go and speak with him. If you finish first, I'll see you and George in the morning."

Moma rapped lightly on Josh's door and entered. The boy sat with his back to the door, "Leave me alone!" he shouted.

Moma closed the door and sat on the boy's bed. "Josh, I know you're angry, but you cannot speak to me that way. This is my home and I will have anyone I want live here. I invited you and Angie to live with me and now I'm inviting your father. He is family and what's more – Angie knew and loved that man."

Josh lowered his head into his hands and wept loudly. Moma pulled him to her and held him.

"I can't believe she's gone," Josh cried.

"That's because she isn't. She's with us always, in our memories and in our hearts. And when this life is over, Angie will be waiting for us," whispered Moma.

"But she's all alone. Angie hated to be alone," sobbed Josh.

Moma held the broken boy tighter and whispered, "She's not alone. She's with your mother and all those who went before her. She's with God and she'll never be alone again."

Josh was inconsolable. "I did it. I let her die and I'll never forgive myself."

Moma paused, allowing the boy a chance to cry. "It seems to me you have a lot of forgiving to do."

Josh pulled away, his anger renewed. "If you mean that man, I'll never forgive him. He left her when she was just a baby, a baby who needed him."

"Oh, and what about Tommy? Can you forgive him?"

Josh seemed stunned by the question. "No, I'll never forgive him. He lured her out on the lake. He wanted to kill her."

"And yet she forgave him. She gave her life to save him." Moma whispered.

Josh's face hardened as he thought of Angie.

"Do you remember when we took that vacation by the shore with Angie? We went to Mass at that little, brown church by the sea?" asked Moma.

"Yes, Angie loved the beach, especially the sailboats," answered Josh.

"Remember that Irish priest, you know, the one from County Kerry? He did that sermon on the book by Dickens. It's called *A Christmas Carol*. He did such a funny rendition of the first ghost that visited Ebenezer Scrooge. Do you remember?"

Josh seemed distracted by the question. "Yes, it was Marley, his old business partner."

"Do you remember how the priest looked as he imitated Marley covered by those heavy chains?"

For the first time in days, Josh smiled. "I remember Angie driving me crazy. Remember how she tied those ropes around her wrists and shoulders? Then she tied rags around her ankles and knees. All day she pretended the ropes were heavy chains. She stumbled all over the bungalow and claimed she couldn't do her chores because she was a ghost full of chains. All night she jumped out from behind chairs and tables yelling 'woo-woo' trying to scare everyone." Josh's face lit with love as he remembered his sister and her antics.

Moma laughed with the memory. "But remember the point of the sermon. Marley was condemned to carry those heavy chains for all of eternity. Those chains dragged along, weighing him down. Those were the chains of unforgiveness." Moma asked, "Do you want to carry such heavy chains for all eternity? Those chains will keep you down, and away from Angie and your mother, and all the people you love in heaven."

Josh seemed crushed. "I can't help it. I hate them for what they did to her. I hate myself because I allowed it all to happen!"

"Let's just forgive one at a time, shall we?" whispered Moma as she held the boy tenderly. "Let's start with your father. Do you think you can forgive him? After all, Angie did."

Josh wept. "I don't think I can. I'm not Angie."

"Can we try? I think we could try for as long as Angie did. Then if it doesn't work, I'll understand and tell him to leave. Okay?" asked Moma.

"Do you promise? Do you promise that if I can't forgive him, he'll have to go?" begged Josh as he looked at his grandmother.

"Yes, I promise. Let's see now. Angie visited Artie one day a week for about a year. That's 52 days. Do you think you could try for 52 days? Maybe, after that, you will be able to forgive him."

Josh didn't want to forgive and knew he never would. But if this was the only way he could get rid of the man, he would agree to try. "Yes, as long as you promise it will only be 52 days."

Moma nodded. "I promise, as long as you pretend to like him and be friends with him."

Josh agreed, resolving it would all be an act. *He could talk to the man and pretend they were friends. Once his time is up, I'll be rid of him for good!* he thought as he wiped his tears.

Moma stood up and announced, "Come then and have something to eat before you go to bed. Artie and George are coming tomorrow."

Moma just smiled when Josh asked, "Hey wait a minute, who's George?"

Twenty

Build up, build up, prepare the way; remove the stumbling blocks from my people's path. For thus says he who is high and living eternally, whose name is the Holy One: On high I dwell, and in holiness and with the crushed and dejected in spirit. To revive the spirits of the dejected, to revive the hearts of the crushed. (Isa. 57: 14-15)

We often get annoyed with the people in our lives. We are exasperated with their habits and disagree with their opinions. We wish they would just stop talking so much or hope they would speak up. Let the moodiness end. Are they going to tell that same story again, we wonder? Can't they stop drumming their fingers on the table or stop chewing that gum so loudly? It's the strangest thing that when we lose them, it is the little annoyances we remember fondly. It is the small habits we miss the most.

Josh woke up to the sound of Moma rattling around in the kitchen. He lay in bed a few moments trying to unravel the truth of what happened yesterday. *I wish it were a nightmare,* thought the boy as he realized Angie would not be at the breakfast table today. She would not be complaining to Moma about wearing a dress to Mass.

Each Sunday like clockwork, Angie would argue with Moma

about the dress, announcing that none of the other girls were forced to wear a dress. She would try to use the logic of not having to change when she got home. Angie would even try the ridiculous ploy of how clean the dress would stay if it was just kept hanging in the closet. Repeatedly every Sunday morning, Angie would replicate the same old arguments, to no avail. Moma always won.

How will I live without her? the boy thought as his eyes welled with tears. *God, how could you take her so soon?* The pain was more than he could bear, but there was nothing he could do. Josh sighed. Angie was gone and he couldn't bring her back.

The boy clung to the familiar. Moma making breakfast was normal. Clinging to normal was all he had left. Washed and dressed he entered the kitchen. Expecting the customary, he found anything but. Moma, wearing her best dress, was wrapping her hotcakes on paper plates for later use.

"What are you doing?" Josh asked.

Moma seemed in a hurry as she prepared to leave. "I have a lot to do. I talked to the funeral director and he said that, because of the inquiry into Angie's death, we wouldn't be able to hold the services until next Saturday. So I think I'll get about other business that needs to be taken care of."

"What business?" Josh couldn't stand the thought of being alone. "Can I go with you?"

"No, your father and George are moving in today. I want you to be here to help him get settled and make sure they eat. I'm leaving some food in the fridge that you can heat up for lunch and there's some chicken for dinner in case I get back late."

The boy's face tightened with emotion. "You're leaving me alone with that man? You're leaving me the day after Angie died? Where are you going?"

Moma finished wrapping the food on the counter and turned to her grandson. "I hate to leave you, but you won't be alone. You'll be with your father. I thought we had this discussion last night."

Josh couldn't believe what he was hearing. "I need to be with

166

you. I need to talk about my sister. Don't you understand? You and I are the only ones left."

"I understand you think that," answered Moma as she buttoned her coat. "That's where you are making your mistake. We are not the only two who miss Angie and need to talk about her. I am aware that you need to talk. Your father also needs to talk. He'll be here any minute. Now I have to go to someone who needs me more than you, someone who has no one to talk to. I'm going to stop for Mass on the way. Please make sure you and your father get to a later Mass."

Josh gave up. In a way, Moma was a lot like Angie. Once she made up her mind, there was no changing it. He was curious about who needed Moma more than he did, but knew he'd only find out when she was ready to share.

Walking over to his grandmother, he wrapped his arms around her. She hugged him tightly and whispered in his ear, "You know I love you. You'll always be first with me. Think of Angie and what she would want you to do. He needs you and she'll be watching from heaven."

Josh sighed as he watched Moma walk out the door. He wasn't sure he could do what Angie would want.

After Mass, Moma walked the five blocks down to the hospital. Stopping at the desk, she asked for Tommy.

"Are you a relative?" asked the woman.

"Yes," answered Moma without hesitation as she took the pass. *He's my brother in Christ*, she thought as she walked toward the elevator.

Tommy lay silently in the pediatric intensive care ward, unaware and alone. Monitors beeped and an intravenous dripped. Moma removed her coat. Pulling the curtains closed around them, she created a private spot. The elderly woman removed the vial of blessed oil she always carried in her purse. She uncapped the vial and, with arthritic hands, anointed the boy on his forehead, then laid the other hand over his heart. The odor of frankincense and myrrh permeated the room.

Raising her eyes to heaven, she prayed aloud. "In the name of Jesus Christ and in the power of the Holy Spirit, I bind the Spirits of Anger, Murder, and Rage and I send them to the foot of the Cross to be dealt with as the Father sees fit."

Moma repeated her prayer three times and then prayed, "May the Holy Spirit come and fill the empty spots in this child's heart, soul, and spirit with his love, peace, and forgiveness, and by that same Holy Spirit heal this boy's body. I thank you Father for a healing you have already given."

Screaming, the Spirits of Murder and Rage spun out of control. The sound of His Name, the Name they never uttered, stabbed them like a knife. They rolled around Tommy's bed like spinning balls set aflame, their tails leaving fiery paths in the air. They wanted to leave, to escape the prayer, but the root spirit clung to the boy.

When the woman, the Woman of Light, called on the Holy Spirit, it was more than the Spirit of Anger could bear. His claws were dug into the boy, clinging with determination. When the Woman of Light praised the Father, his talons weakened. Anger could not hold on and stand in the light. Even though the woman whispered her prayer, her praise of God the Father was so loud and powerful that the Spirit of Anger lost his grip. When he let go, all three of the spirits spun wildly, out of control. Screaming in pain, they disappeared in a puff of smoke – sent to the Cross.

A light, a golden light came and bathed the woman and the boy hidden behind the curtains. The nurses carried on with their chores, the doctors wrote their orders, the other patients talked to their visitors, all unaware of the battle that had just been fought and won.

The angels watched and, as they sang praises to the God of the Universe; a crescendo of music filled the room, unheard by the human ear. A light had come with the woman, the light of heaven. All the dark spirits lurking in the corners of the intensive care unit shrieked and disappeared.

Taking a chair beside his bed, she sat by the boy who remained in a coma and started to talk in a soft, low voice. She didn't speak about anything special. She just spoke about the town, the events of the day. Later that afternoon, Moma pulled out her Bible and read passages to the unresponsive child. The nurses who passed by thought she must be an old aunt or grandmother. No one questioned her reason for being there. Moma came each morning for the next week and sat beside the boy for the entire day. Each time she continued to whisper softly or gently read the psalms. The only day she didn't come was Saturday, the day of Angie's funeral.

On Saturday morning, people started to enter St. Veronica's church. The stained-glass windows filtered prisms of light, which splashed across the walls and pews of the inner sanctum. The Mass was scheduled for ten, but the church was full to capacity fifteen minutes early. Harold entered with Ruthie and wore his best pinstripe suit. His face was full of pain and Ruthie dabbed her eyes.

Mrs. Lennon arrived early, with her neighbor Mrs. Larsen beside her. She had made it a point to ask Inga if she would accompany her, stating, "I hate to go to these things alone. I feel uncomfortable walking in by myself. You'd be doing me a great favor if you would ride over there with me."

Inga knew what her neighbor was really doing. She was making sure that Inga wouldn't be too afraid to attend. Inga Larsen appreciated the kindness. She accepted the invitation without hesitation. Inga was becoming aware of the little kindnesses of others.

Father Hogan dressed slowly in the sacristy. He had officiated many funeral Masses in his day, but this one was going to be difficult. Children's funerals always were, but this one was going to be especially hard because he was so attached to little Angie. He had carefully selected some readings, hoping to ease the pain of those in attendance.

Tien Ca' Le came with Logan. She tried to talk the boy out of coming, believing children should not attend funerals. Death was something that should not concern children. *Children are about life, not death*, she thought as she walked in with the small boy. Logan had insisted Angie was his friend. She had saved him and he wanted to thank her by coming. Tien knew how many losses the boy had suffered and couldn't refuse him. *He had a need to say good-bye to Angie and who was she to deny him that right?*

Reverend Huber found a seat right behind Tien. He couldn't take his eyes off her. Her delicate movements and graceful hands mesmerized him. He pondered how he would talk to her. Watching her experienced, gentle handling of the small, blond boy who sat beside her, he realized that she must work with children. *Maybe she's a teacher*, he thought. *Could that be how she knew Angie?*

Thinking of Angie pulled his thoughts back to the present. Today they would bury that precious child who had touched so many lives. Looking around the church, seeing the numerous faces of the people who cared about Angie, Reverend Huber was astonished by how many people had loved the child. She had touched so many lives during her short time on earth. She had brought love to more people than many who had a full lifetime.

The church was full when everyone stood for the entrance. Moma, Josh, and Artie followed the small casket up the center aisle as Angie's favorite hymn, *Be Not Afraid*, played. Sitting in the first pew, Angie's family watched as Harold walked to the podium to lector the first reading from Revelation.

"For this reason they stand before God's throne and worship Him day and night in His temple. The One who sits on the throne will shelter them. They will not hunger or thirst anymore, nor will the sun or any heat strike them. For the Lamb who is in the center of the throne will shepherd them and lead them to springs of life-giving water, and God will wipe away every tear from their eyes."

Father Hogan read the gospel. "When He saw the crowds, He went up the mountain, and after He had sat down, His disciples came to Him. He began to teach them, saying:

"Blessed are the poor in spirit,
For theirs is the kingdom of heaven.
Blessed are they who mourn,
For they will be will be comforted.
Blessed are the meek,
For they will inherit the land.
Blessed are they who hunger and thirst
For righteousness,
For they will be satisfied.
Blessed are the merciful,
For they will be shown mercy.
Blessed are the clean of heart,
For they will see God.
Blessed are the peacemakers,
For they will be called children of God.
Blessed are they who are persecuted
For the sake of righteousness,
For theirs is the kingdom of heaven,

Blessed are you when they insult you and persecute you and utter every kind of evil against you (falsely) because of Me. Rejoice and be glad, for your reward will be great in heaven. Thus they persecuted the prophets who were before you."

Father Hogan paused before he gave a short and simple homily. "Angie was all the things that Christ calls us to be in the Beatitudes. She lived the Beatitudes. Therefore, she is now at peace with Christ." The Mass continued, simple and direct. It eased the pain of the people who loved Angie.

A reception followed at Moma's house after the burial and, despite the sorrow, there was much laughter as the stories of Angie's numerous antics were told. It was balm to the wound, but Moma was exhausted.

Inga Larson went to the kitchen to get her a drink and noticed Logan standing by the window. Her heart stopped and she stood staring in amazement. When Tien entered, she grabbed her and asked, "Who is that boy? He looks just like my Karl when he was that age."

Tien smiled and, as she told Logan's story, Inga could not take her eyes off the child. The Lord moves in mysterious ways, Tien thought as she introduced Logan to the woman.

The day after Angie's funeral, Moma got up early, dressed, and headed to the hospital before Josh or Artie even arose. The man and his newly found son had spent everyday together since Angie's death and seemed to be developing a relationship. Her best contribution was to get out of the way.

Never stand in the way of the Holy Spirit, she thought as she again sat beside Tommy's bed. This time, out of the corner of her eye, she noticed movement. Tommy turned his head and opened his eyes.

Moma smiled and said, "Well, hello. I see that you're waking up."

The boy stared at her. "Who are you?"

Moma smiled. "I'm Angie's grandmother. Everyone calls me Moma."

At the mention of Angie's name, Tommy reddened, and in a whisper asked, "How is she?"

"She's with her Father," Moma answered, thinking that the truth should always be given gently.

Tommy seemed relieved. "She's lucky to have a father. I wish I had one."

Moma reached over and took the boy's hand. "Ah ... but you do. Why, you're the spitting image of your Father."

Tommy stared. "You know my father?"

"Yes," Moma answered, "I do know your Father."

Tommy's face tightened as he turned away. "I don't know him

and it doesn't matter. He's no good and neither am I. I'm just like him. I bet you hate him and you'll hate me, too. Everybody does."

Moma reached over and gently touched Tommy's chin, turning his face toward her. "I know your Father and He's nothing like that. He's loving, creative, kind, and generous."

Tommy couldn't believe his ears. "You really do know him, don't you?"

"I do," answered Moma. "Would you like me to tell you about your Father?"

Epilogue
(One Year Later)

The true light, which enlightens everyone, was coming into the world. He was in the world, and the world came to be through him, but the world did not know him. He came to what was his own, but his own people did not accept him. But to those who did accept him, he gave power to become children of God, to those who believe in his name, who were born not by natural generation nor by human choice nor by a man's decision, but of God. And the Word became flesh and made his dwelling among us, and we saw his glory, the glory as of the Father's only Son, full of grace and truth. (John 1: 9-14)

Moma was in pain. The arthritis had gotten worse in the year since Angie's death. She felt herself slowing down. *Will you be taking me home soon, Jesus? I want to see my daughter, Julia, and Angie. I want to see my husband and parents, but most of all, I want to see You.*

Moma poured another cup of batter onto the heated griddle. Angie had always loved waffles on Saturday morning. Tommy loved them also. Today she had to make a big batch. It was opening day of trout fishing. Her men and boys had gotten up early and were at the lake trying their luck. She knew they would be famished when they got home. She had gotten up at sunrise to prepare the meal. Pulling the now-done waffle from the iron with a fork, Moma poured the last of the batter to form a sort of half-waffle.

She had just put the plate of finished waffles up on the stove, out of reach, when the front door opened and George came bounding into the kitchen. Jumping up and down in front of Moma, he let his large tongue hang from his mouth, his sign of hunger.

Laughing, the elderly woman pulled the last bit of waffle off of the iron and tossed it to the black lab. He immediately took his treat under the table to enjoy as the men entered the kitchen.

"Eww," Moma exclaimed as the strong smell of fish accompanied them. "You'd better all wash up before breakfast."

Tommy held a bucket and, with his eyes aglow, announced, "Here are the fish. I caught the biggest one!"

Moma couldn't believe the change in the boy. He had not only grown a few inches taller, he had filled out. His now plump face was somehow so much softer than the dark angular face of his past.

Josh laughed as he affirmed Tommy's statement. "He actually caught the biggest trout I'd ever seen come out of that lake."

Moma laughed with delight and, turning to Artie and Father Hogan, asked, "Will you be staying for some breakfast, Father?"

Taking a deep inspiration of breath, Father Hogan answered, "Well, if that's waffles I smell, I will have to stay, won't I?"

"Two or three waffles?" Moma asked as she took down the plates from the cabinet. Tommy had returned from washing up in the bathroom and set the kitchen table with utensils, syrup, and butter.

"Better make it one," Father answered as he patted his rounded stomach, "I've put on a bit of weight this year. Mrs. Lennon, God love her, brings me over at least two casseroles a week. I've been eating like a king. Now I have a king's gut."

Moma served the meal as the men and boys sat around the table reminiscing about their great catch. Moma noticed the glow of contentment on Tommy's face.

Artie laughed as Tommy reached for his third waffle. "Better slow down, son. We have a wedding feast ahead of us."

"Yes," announced Father as he got up to leave, "I better go and check on the church. Tien is so nervous about the details. Everything needs to be perfect. I don't know how Reverend Huber has managed to keep her calm."

"What's perfect is the marriage. I've never seen two people so much in love," announced Moma.

"This is my second wedding since I came home," added Artie, "I hope the food is as good as it was at Ruthie and Harold's wedding. Hey Tommy, we better clean these fish and refrigerate them. We won't be able to enjoy them till tomorrow."

Tommy looked worried and Josh picked right up on his concern. "Go and get ready for your deliveries," Josh offered. "I'll help Dad clean the fish."

Tommy bounded, with George right beside him, into the living room to fold the bundle of newspapers.

Tommy had taken over the paper route that Angie so loved. It hadn't been easy. The townspeople had a long memory and a difficult time forgiving the young boy. Most of them turned a cold shoulder to Tommy. Some couldn't contain their contempt of him.

They sometimes mumbled in his presence, mumbled loud enough for him to hear. Others didn't mute their distain. They called him names. Horrible names like "killer" or "white trash." About three days a week, Tommy would come home and dissolve into tears over the cruel words he'd heard from people in town. Then Moma would take him in her arms and talk to him about his heavenly Father. It would calm the boy.

One night when he was especially broken over an adult calling him "trash", Moma was inspired with a poem. At first Tommy thought it was just too silly. Later, when he heard that word again, he repeated it.

"Whether I'm poor or whether I have cash, my heavenly Father doesn't make trash."

The adult, taken by surprise, took his paper and just slammed the door. Somehow it made Tommy feel vindicated.

The next week when some of the children at school called him a killer, Tommy was quick to respond. Looking directly at the bullies, he announced, "You can kill with your words, you can kill with your mind, but the Lord Jesus Christ was always so kind."

Within a year, the town's acceptance seemed to grow and Tommy became a welcome part of the community. He continued to make his rounds each Saturday, bringing local news to individuals. His presence alone seemed a lesson to many.

Josh and Artie made short order of cleaning the fish in the kitchen sink as Moma wiped up the last remnants of breakfast.

"I better get going also," Artie said. "I'm supposed to be at the airport in an hour. I don't want to make that elderly woman wait for me – not after that long flight from Vietnam."

"Tien's going to be so thrilled to have her birth mother sitting in the church," said Moma. "I love this town and the people in it. It was so good of the townsfolk to raise the money to fly Tien's mother over for the wedding. I can't wait to see the look on Tien's face."

"It doesn't surprise me," announced Father Hogan as he stood by the kitchen door, preparing to leave. "Tien has spent years taking care of the children of this town. Everyone here loves her. The town felt as if it was the least they could do in return. I can't wait for Tien to see her.

"You should see our church. I've never seen so many flowers. It seems everyone in the town wanted to contribute their part. It's going to be a beautiful wedding. And Mrs. Larsen is paying for the reception. I can't believe the change in that woman since she took Logan in. It's as if she's come back to life. Becoming a foster mother has changed her life."

Father Hogan headed for the church and the final preparations for the wedding of Reverend Huber and Tien Ca' Le. In the driveway, Artie revved up the engine of his secondhand car. He had a long drive to the airport. With the two men on their separate missions, Tommy finished folding the papers and putting them in the basket of his bike.

Jumping excitedly, George, the boy's constant companion, was waiting at the front door, ready to go. Josh let the dog out to join Tommy on his rounds. Angie's old route had doubled in size, but

Tommy could finish in half the time. He could probably do it even faster if he wanted to, but he, like Angie, often stopped to visit the people along the way. Even though it had taken a painfully long time for the town to accept him, it now seems as if he had always belonged.

Moma and Josh watched from the picture window as Tommy started up the block on his bike, with George running beside him.

"He looks so happy, doesn't he?" Moma asked.

"He's so proud! You should have seen him when he caught that fish," Josh answered. "Hold on, I got a picture of it."

Josh ran into to kitchen to get his camera and, returning, pushed some buttons as he scanned through the photos. "Here it is. See, he pulled that trout right out of the water as the sun rose."

Moma looked at the picture. The trout's silver skin sparkled in the golden glow of the sunrise. It was a magnificent picture.

"Look, you can see the sunrise," bragged Josh, as he stared at his camera. "The sun was just coming up."

Moma gently smiled. "Yes, Josh. Never forget. The Son is Risen!"

About Author
Karen Kelly Boyce

Karen Kelly Boyce was born in Jersey City, New Jersey. She learned her faith and love of reading at the hands of the Sisters of Mercy. Only a few blocks away from the Barron Library, she spent most of her summer days and weekends lost in the stories and biographies of famous people. The turbulent sixties led her away from her first loves of church, reading, and writing. The only part of her faith that remained was the belief that we were made to help others. That belief led her to graduate as an RN in 1974.

Karen married in 1975, and raised two children. After going through a Life in the Spirit Seminar, she found peace and eternal love in the faith that would sustain her. In 1990, she became very ill and was eventually diagnosed with end stage Lyme Disease and was unable to work as a nurse anymore. As a disabled person, Karen's love of reading was rekindled and her love of writing born again.

Karen is the author of three other books - *Into the Way of Peace, According to Thy Word* and a *Bend in the Road: A Year's Journey Through Breast Cancer*; all of which have received the esteemed Catholic Writers Guild seal of approval.

All books can be purchased on line at :

www.queenofangelsfarm.com or
www.jacksonwritersgroup.com/boyce.html

Made in the USA
San Bernardino, CA
09 November 2013